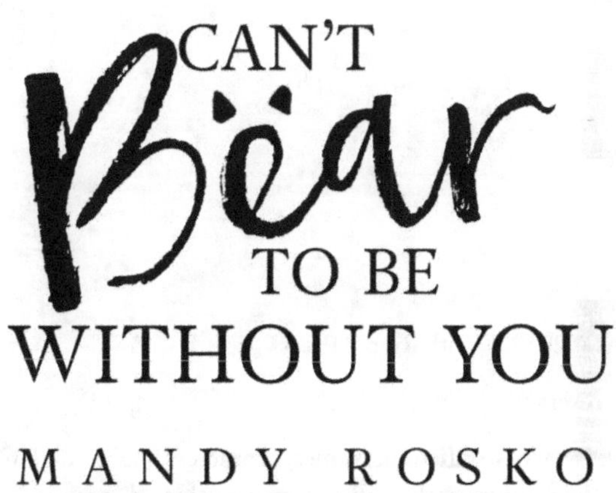

CAN'T Bear TO BE WITHOUT YOU

MANDY ROSKO

Cover art by Yocla Book Cover Designs

Edited by Brieanna Robertson, Beth Fawcett, and Jessica Ripley

Published by Eighth Ripple Press

Print ISBN: 978-0-9950867-7-7

Ebook ISBN: 978-0-9950867-8-4

CONTENTS

*This book is dedicated to all of my patrons over on Patreon!
Thank you for your continuous support! - Mandy*

*Nancy Mcdonald, Tami Gryder, Jessica Ripley, Nicole Henry,
Barbara Burdette, Johanna Snodgrass, Andi Downs, Alisha
Derr, Nicole Cook, Michelle Fortune, Teresa Ward, Sherry
Smith, Angie Kyle, Melinda Miller, Leslie Gordon, Saleena
Chamberlin, Ramona Cabrera, Dusty Weller, Terri Eaches.*

*Daria Donnelly, Kayla Reindl, Clare Parrott, Patricia Cassar,
Sheryl Tegtmeyer, Lori Martin, Anne Rindfliesch, Stacy Itter-
sagen, Megan Mills, Christina Morgan, Monica Lynn Emery,
Leanne Ede, Cassandra Hyden.*

*Anne Samson, Pauline Dixon, Rachelle Binkley, Rebekah
Snyder, Michelle Chantler, Thomas Werner, Kaer Baer,
Sharron Anthony, Roxanne Johnson, Rachel Morse, Karen,
Marlene Eaton, Julie Spencer, Wendy Custer, Annette Alex,
Shelia Deal, Carolyn Lown, Mellissa, Jill Micklich, Confused
Child, Samalee Johnson, Sandy Folz, Janet Rodman, Jeanne
Clark, David Friend.*

Lizzy, Soshanahlila, Alexandra Smith, Virginia Robinson,

Donna Hogel, Nanci Quinn, Janice Richmond, Stacey F, Barb Sands, Marcy Schwendiman, Charlotte Brincat, Sharon Manning-Lew, Teresa Albarran, Gerryann L., Denise Holder, Gail Powell, Rose Allen.

Opal Carew Lori Trask, Retiredhsmom, Maria T, Rachel Barckhaus, Laura Furuta, Angela Cowen, Diana Mason, Beth Wolfe, Toni Mcconnell, Valerie Cobb, Valerie Jondahl.

Tiffany Villeda, Iona Stewart, Samantha Quinones, Seen Cassell, Melissa Carlton, Ugo, Amanda Barker, Tricha Fely, Corrina Mayall, Ellen Swindall-Bailey, Alexis Abbott, Selena Kitt, Essie Munro, Anna Garcia-Centner, Biggi Ziegler, Jill Morrison, Alexia Falco, Kerrin Brittain, Ruth Roberts, Carol Ingham, Cynthia Powers, Tanya, Yolanda Pedroza, Belinda Jarrell, Miriam Loellgen, Pam Van Veen, Tammy Francis, Valerie Marshman.

Jonas MacBride left Lakeview in his past, including the woman who spurned him. There was no place there for a subhuman like him – someone born to shifters without the ability to transform. Yet after years of building a life for himself, and a career as a firefighter, he's sent back to Lakeview to investigate some recent brushfire incidents. And on his first day in town he runs right into the woman he once thought he'd spend his life with.

Taylor Daniella Norina thought she'd seen the last of Jonas until he shows up asking questions about fires – questions that none of the shifter community is interested in answering. She can tell that Jonas doesn't want to be there, and she'd prefer he left as soon as possible too. Someone might be hiding the truth about who's setting the brushfires, but Taylor has her own secret – one involving the child she carried when Jonas left her behind.

Can't Bear to Be Without You is book 3 in the You've Got to be Shifting Me series.

Zero Fox Given
Howl Always Love You
Can't Bear to Be Without You

CHAPTER 1

Jonas MacBride walked into the building with a sense of trepidation he wasn't used to. He'd rushed into house fires with more enthusiasm than this. He tried not to show it, but there was something about a woman, this woman, that was wilder, brighter, and deadlier than any fire.

Also, his size seventeen boots didn't feel as though they belonged anywhere near a child's daycare center. He noted the sign on the front door, reading the times for play, snacks, and naps.

And right about now, it was nap time.

He made it to the front desk, where a small sign with the words, "ring for service" sat, but he didn't ring it.

Seriously? Why have that there at all? Someone should be monitoring the front entrance of a place with so many little kids around.

Jonas grit his teeth. He wanted to turn and walk right out of there, maybe come back another time, perhaps when all the little wet and crying bundles were hoisted off onto their parents.

Or somewhere else entirely.

Not that he didn't like kids. He liked them. He liked it when there were school trips to his firehouse and he got to show them all the cool equipment and see something akin to hero worship in their eyes. But even the bored ones were better to deal with than babies.

Jonas didn't know what to do with the particularly small ones.

And Taylor owned this place? He hadn't figured her as one for taking care of other people's kids, but he supposed it was a living.

In a place like Lakeview, there weren't too many options for people looking to drop off their shifter kids for the day. With so many packs and skulks, and even sloths, living around here, this place was probably a good idea. But considering how hard it was for shifters to get daycare for their kids in communities of mostly non-shifters, and the fighting that went on between breeds... it stunned him something like this could function at all.

Jonas checked his watch. About five minutes in. She might have forgotten he was coming. Or maybe she'd hoped he wouldn't come.

He was not touching that damned bell. If he did, and some little kid woke up from the noise, he'd be damned if the crying was blamed on him.

Did Taylor have a boyfriend? His mind wandered back to the thought that drifted into his mind on his way over here… in between the other things he'd been thinking of.

He snapped back to where he was when the door to his left opened wide. Taylor Daniella Norina stepped out, took one look at him, and froze mid-step. Light from the window bathed her hair and made it gleam and shine. Her skin looked smoother than he remembered, and her mouth much pinker.

He could remember the things she'd done with that mouth, and the only reason he didn't play with those thoughts was because of where he stood.

He smiled at her. "I figured you knew it wasn't me."

She blinked, coming out of whatever spell had taken her, checked behind her, and closed the door. Not before Jonas could tilt his head to the side and see for himself all the little bundles sleeping on their mats.

"How many are you handling?"

She shut the door quietly, as though worried she would wake a beast. "Enough." She turned to look at him, crossing her arms. "What are you doing here?"

Jonas blew out a hard breath. "That's cold."

She pressed her lips together, her fingers digging into her arm. "What are you doing here, Jonas?"

It was cold, but there was a hint of something else he couldn't place. Worry? About what?

He smiled. "You think I'm coming to beg for you back?"

She shrugged. "You show up out of the blue, what am I supposed to think?"

"Hardly out of the blue. I wanted to check up on some things. Completely friendly. This isn't to be pathetic and come begging for your attention. You made it clear you didn't want me around." He couldn't keep the edge out of his voice. He knew it was a mistake to remind her of anything regarding their relationship, and how it ended, when he watched her inhale a sharp breath.

"You should go."

"I need to have a word with you."

"I have an appointment right now. When he walks in here, I won't have time for you."

"With Dallas Burns?"

Taylor jerked back, her long, thick lashes fanning as she blinked. "How do you know about that?"

He shrugged, knowing he was about to give her some news she wouldn't like. "He sent me in his place."

"Sent you... you know him?"

"Yeah, he's kind of my boss."

Her shoulders sagged.

He wanted to laugh at her for that. "Don't look too happy for me or anything."

Taylor shook her head. "No, I mean... I'm sorry. That's good. It's what you always wanted. To be a firefighter, right?"

"Yeah. Not doing too badly either."

He was proud to admit it. He'd been in the middle of training when they were dating, but being out here, with not much going on...and debating whether or not he wanted to get married and have kids with the woman he loved...

"So, have you been fighting a lot of fires lately?"

"Eh." He shrugged, making a seesawing motion with his hand. "Not really. My first two times out were to help a woman who called us to tell us her entire house was lit up."

"That's...pretty terrible. Was she all right?"

He snorted a laugh. "Yeah. Her house was fine too. Her dog just got stuck beneath the porch. She wanted our help getting it out." He'd been spitting mad at the time, but looking back, it was kind of funny. "Second time out was a call from an older guy who called us saying he couldn't breathe. Turned out he couldn't breathe through his nose, but air was going through his mouth just fine. When we got there, the only thing we could do was offer to take him to the hospital. He didn't want to go, so we left."

Taylor smiled, and that was good. That was all Jonas wanted at that moment. He didn't even know he wanted it until he saw it, but God, her smile was just as pretty as he remembered.

"Well, at least no one was hurt?"

"Speak for yourself. I caught that cold."

She laughed out loud, quickly stopping herself and looking back at the closed door.

They were both silent for a few seconds, waiting to hear if any of the toddlers inside would wake up. None did from the sounds of it.

They both breathed a relieved sigh.

When Taylor looked back at him, Jonas found himself strangely lost in her eyes. He couldn't help but remember all of the good times. The plans they'd made. How it felt to touch the warmth of her skin.

Even with the way things had ended, it wasn't enough to dampen his memories of her.

And make him yearn for those times to come back.

But they wouldn't. She didn't want a future with a subhuman. She'd made that clear.

He shoved those feelings away, and fast, trying not to look at the cute little rounded ears on either side of her head. The ears that looked like those of a black bear. "So, how have you been?"

Taylor pushed a strand of hair out of her face, one of

those ears twitching. He used to play with those ears in bed. They were very ticklish.

"Fine. Everything's been...great."

"Everything?"

She went back to crossing her arms, not a good sign. "Everything with the exception of the fires. I guess that's what you're here for?"

He nodded. "Something like that. My captain will be coming around to ask some questions of the local business owners, too. You might hear from him later."

"But he sent you for this meeting?"

He nodded. "Yeah."

She seemed to think about that. "Is that even allowed?"

"How do you mean?"

"Well, you and I have a history together. Isn't it a conflict of interest or something to have you come and question me about the fires when someone else could do it?"

"Which is why this isn't exactly official." He looked at her, wishing he could make her understand, wishing he knew what was going on inside that head of hers.

"You're not in any trouble, and I'm not a cop. I just wanted to make sure you're all right."

She pressed her lips together. "Does your captain know you know me?"

"He does."

She nodded. "And he still sent you?"

"He hoped that knowing you would allow me to get some honest answers. This is a shifter community, not too many people around here want to speak to anyone human, or subhuman."

She cringed.

Right. She hated that word. Hated the reminder of what he was.

He didn't have the ears and tail. He was born into a shifter community, and yet he couldn't shift. Few shifters wanted something like that for breeding. Not if there was a chance it could taint a bloodline and bring about cubs who couldn't shift either.

Shifters were a little too extreme on making sure their population remained steady, almost to the point of paranoia.

Some called the declining shifter population genocide. But some people also thought the Earth was flat, the sun revolved around the Earth, and lizard people ruled the government. All kinds of nonsense.

He would have never thought Taylor would end up being one of those people.

"We're just trying to make sure no one gets hurt. That's all we're doing. Looking out for you, your alpha, those babies in there." He pointed to the door.

Taylor glanced back at it, as though she could see the little ones inside.

A look came over her face that he couldn't exactly read. He watched her, waiting for her to give her response, hoping desperately that it would be the one he wanted to hear the most.

"Andrew won't like it if I'm talking to you."

So, Andrew was still her alpha. Made sense, the guy was the steady sort — someone with a good head on his shoulders.

The kind of guy Jonas used to look up to.

"Do you have only bears in that room? Or are there some wolves? Foxes? A few coyotes, maybe?"

"I take care of any shifter children who need me to watch them."

He nodded. "Right, so the packs can get along when they need to."

"This isn't about getting along."

"Taylor, someone is setting fires out here. Big ones. We've been lucky so far that the local teams have been able to put them out, but it won't be long before I get called in to help."

Concern seemed to flitter across her eyes. "No, that won't happen. You're in the city."

"You think we won't get called in if another big fire hits? It took three days to put out the last one, and if it hadn't rained, it could have been much worse. That fire was getting a little too close to your territory. We know someone's doing this. If it's a dispute between alphas, please let me know. I don't want you hurt, and I don't want those kids in there hurt. I know you don't either."

Again, she bit her lips together, but this time, Jonas could tell he had her.

"What do you want to know?"

He sighed, relaxing, taking in the small victory. "Do you or your alpha know who's behind this?"

She looked him dead in the eyes. "No, we don't."

His ire rose right up again. He couldn't help it, and Jonas clenched his hands into fists. "You're a terrible liar."

CHAPTER 2

Taylor heaved a sigh as she locked the door to her daycare.

It took the McKormicks an hour longer than usual to come and pick up Danny, which meant she was getting out of here at almost six in the afternoon.

She did have an extra fee, charged by the hour whenever someone happened to pull that sort of stunt on her, but at the same time, she knew the situation of the McKormicks, which meant she knew the chances of being paid that extra time were slim.

She might get lucky, however. Sometimes, they paid her. Other times, they seemed to forget they had any outstanding payments due at all, and she didn't want to fight with them over what they did or did not owe to her.

It wasn't worth the extra twenty-five dollars sometimes.

Meg slept nicely against her chest, however. That was a good thing. She'd had a snack with Danny while they waited for his parents, but it wasn't the same things as a proper dinner for a one-and-a-half-year-old.

Thank God Jonas hadn't seen her. If he had...

Taylor shook her head, moving to her car. He wasn't going to know. She worked in a daycare, so of course it wouldn't look odd to him to see Meg.

She was still a baby.

But she looked so much like her father.

Taylor buckled Meg into her car seat in the back of her car. She shut the door, sighing at the rusted flakes that were coming off at the bottom.

Probably not the safest vehicle in the world for her pride and joy, but it got the job done.

She'd tried to open her daycare at home, but coyotes, wolves, foxes, and even other bears weren't willing to step into territory that was not their own, let alone leave their children behind on it.

Neutral territory was the only way to go, it seemed, and even that was something she could barely get away with. Some parents were still not convinced about leaving their young with her, especially with other breeds of shifters around. The ones who did tended to be parents like the McKormicks, people who had little choice if they wanted to work. She kept her prices reasonably low, was able to thanks to the number of children she did have, and the only extra thing she asked was that parents provide their snacks. In return, she would keep a safe environment for their children.

The drive home was uneventful, though Jonas came back to mind when she passed by the result of one of the recent smaller fires. The dead, charcoal remains of the pines looked like skeletal hands. She was used to seeing the trees bare in the winter, but blackened like that, and standing next to half-burned maples and birch trees was... off-putting, to say the least.

When she got home, she didn't park at her trailer. She went straight to Andrew's house, knocking on his door while holding Meg in her arms. She knew he was home. His lights were on, and she could smell him inside.

She banged her fist on the wood again, waiting for him to open up.

Taylor heard a grumbling inside, then a small bang, followed by cursing the likes of which she wasn't sure she wanted her daughter to listen to, even in her sleep.

Finally, the door opened.

Andrew's glare melted away when he realized it was Taylor standing there. "Oh, did you want to come in?"

She smiled at him. "You stub your toe?"

He shook his head, growling as he opened the screen and stepped away from the door. "Eyes going in my old age."

Taylor smiled, stepped inside, but then she couldn't smile anymore. "Jonas came to see me at work today."

"Who?"

It didn't sound like he was pretending, and that annoyed her. "Jonas. You know? Jonas? Meg's father?"

He looked at her suddenly, eyes wide. "No shit?"

She glared at him.

"She's sleeping, give me a break."

"You're lucky you're the man in charge."

He smiled at her. "You're lucky you're a favorite."

She didn't feel like a favorite. She hadn't felt that way in a long time. But she wasn't his daughter, his niece, granddaughter, or related to him by blood in any way, so what right did she have to complain about not being given special treatment?

"Jonas is here, and he wants me to tell him who's starting the fires."

"So? We don't know who's starting them. Well, not for sure anyway."

"I told him that."

He looked at her, a note of panic in his eyes. "You told him?"

She shook her head. "No, not like that. He asked me if I had any ideas, if I knew of any territory disputes or pack fights. I said I didn't know."

Andrew nodded. "Good," He headed for the kitchen. "You want something to drink?"

"Water would be great if you have it."

She felt as rough as though she'd just run a marathon. Thank God tomorrow was Saturday. It meant a little less than half of her usual group. She could take it easy. Sunday was the only day she kept the daycare closed. Some of the parents wanted it open, but not enough to justify the cost of keeping the doors open. Plus, she wanted that time alone with Meg.

But with Jonas around, she felt like hiding away entirely. She didn't want to go in to the daycare tomorrow at all.

Andrew handed her the glass of water just as Taylor sat herself down at his small kitchen table.

"Did Jonas say anything about..." He trailed off, vaguely pointing with one hand to Meg.

Taylor drank her water, shaking her head. "No. I don't think he saw her. If he did, he must have thought she belonged to one of the other parents."

She hadn't let him in to see the kids. He hadn't asked either. Most likely because he wasn't there for that, but she had caught the way he'd tilted his head to the side when she'd shut the door. There was a small chance he'd seen Meg, but again, if he had, there was no way he could know she was hers.

Which brought her to her next problem.

"I need to ask you a favor."

"Shoot."

"I need you, or anyone else who has the time, to watch over Meg tomorrow."

"What? Why?" He looked at Meg, still sleeping against Taylor's chest, as though she was about to grow a second head and attack him.

Taylor glared at him. "I'm pretty sure you can handle anything she throws at you."

"Don't be so sure about that."

"You've got to be kidding me. You're a grizzly bear."

"And you want to put an infant into my claws? Right. Not happening."

"What? Why?"

"I don't mix well with kids, and I've got other priorities to see to. Like meeting up with the other pack leaders. The wolves and foxes and the like. They haven't been happy in a while, and I want to make sure things keep running smoothly."

Because things had been running like shit lately. The foxes and the wolves had been going at it ever since someone outright murdered the pack leader of a wolf pack nearby. There was a conduit around, too, and that threw a wrench into everything for a while.

Taylor had never been around a conduit before. They

were supposed to throw off a super potent scent that called for anyone and everyone to mate with them. The children they produced were alphas or something. She couldn't keep all the rumors straight. Especially now, with some idiot starting fires.

Lakeview hadn't precisely been safe as of late. First the murder, then packs fighting over a conduit, and now this?

"Maybe we should let the humans in on this," Taylor thought out loud.

"No."

"They could probably help us put this to bed before anything else happens."

"They'll also splatter this all over their local and national news and peg us for savage monsters. We're dealing with this on our own."

"They already think we're savage monsters. Letting them in to help us might be the best move. Some of the police are shifters anyway. Some of them are subhumans. Like Jonas."

"Subhumans are worse than actual humans." Andrew sat across from her at the table. "They get up their own asses like you wouldn't believe."

She looked at him. "Jonas didn't."

"Oh no? He was the one who didn't want shifter babies."

She cringed, stroking the soft strands of her daughter's hair.

"Thought I wouldn't remember that, did you?"

Taylor grit her teeth. She wouldn't dare glare at her sloth leader, so she glared down at his table, struggling against the burn in her eyes.

"Ah, shit. Look, I'm sorry, but it wasn't me that did this to you."

"I know."

She wanted to be angry with him, but she couldn't be. She tried to tell him that Jonas wasn't that bad. It wasn't his fault, and he wasn't cruel. He hadn't walked out on her for being pregnant. He hadn't known in the first place, and she was too much of a coward to tell him, and couldn't consider terminating the pregnancy, even though she'd been scared of raising Meg on her own.

And thank God she hadn't. Holding her daughter in her arms made everything worth it.

Taylor just never thought she would see Jonas again. When he left, she'd been under the impression he would never come back. The way he spoke to her, even pretending it was all right, that it was for the best that she didn't want to be with him, she could tell he was angry. She knew how much he hated her for breaking his heart.

But it was for the best. Jonas didn't want to be tied down, and didn't want babies, especially if there was the chance they would be shifters.

With Meg's little bear ears and her tiny tail, everyone who saw her would know what she was.

If Jonas saw her now, he'd be pissed.

No, forget that. He'd be outright furious. He'd want to know why she'd kept this from him, and she wouldn't be able to escape the blame for that.

He might even be angry that Meg was a shifter, and Taylor couldn't handle that. The little girl should never feel disdain from her father.

"Maybe you should tell him."

"What?" Taylor's outburst was so strong she jostled

Meg, whose face scrunched up. The starting of a cry sounded, and Taylor knew she was in for it now.

"He's the father. He should know."

Taylor wanted to laugh. "You're the one who said I shouldn't tell him."

He nodded. "Right, that was back when you were considering not carrying the child at all. She's here now. You chose to have her, and now her father is running around out there, and he doesn't know."

This time, she did glare at him, and she didn't give a damn that he was in charge of her position on his territory either. "You're supposed to be on my side here."

He nodded again, and she found herself wishing he would stop doing that because she didn't want to deal with him pretending to be so wise right now.

"I'm on your side. I was on your side when you came crying to me because Jonas didn't want a baby. I was here for you when the elders told you to get rid of the child. I was here for you when you decided to keep it, and I was there for you when you wanted to open your daycare."

Taylor winced. "I know. I'm sorry." Without his loan, she wouldn't have been able to afford the lot to open up her daycare. She would have been stuck here, trying to convince people from other packs that it was all right to leave their children with her.

Which they would not have done. She could see that now.

"I can sense a 'but' in there."

She wished he wouldn't sense anything. "I wish you would have been more than a shoulder to cry on when I broke up with Jonas. When I nearly..."

She didn't like talking about it at all, let alone when

Meg was in her arms now. She never wanted her daughter to know that doing away with the pregnancy had been something she'd considered.

Andrew's expression was cold. There was little to no sympathy in his eyes for her. She wanted to hide away from that look, but of course, she couldn't. It felt like being stared down at with disappointment by her father.

"I didn't advise you one way or the other because it was your life and you were an adult. You could make your own decisions. If you chose not to have Meg, that was up to you. If you wanted to give her up for adoption because you weren't ready, also up to you. If you wanted to keep her, then that was going to be on no one but you. It was the same with Jonas. That wasn't my decision to make for you. He didn't want babies, you were pregnant, and the elders advised you to get rid of him. If you're regretting that now then that's on no one but you."

"But the elders told me—"

"No." He raised a finger, his tone firm as he stopped her. "No. You don't get to do that. The elders don't tell anyone to do anything. That is not their job. I wasn't there, but I know for a fact that is not what they did. They advised you. If you felt persuaded, then that's on you. You weren't a child. You were old enough to make up your mind. Jonas is back now, so you have to think about the decisions you made."

That was so not fair. She couldn't help it. He was right. She knew that deep down; certainly, no one had forced her to do anything she didn't want to do. But at the same time, it was still lousy advice they'd given her.

There was the chance he wouldn't have walked away from her.

Of course, now that she could see what he'd become, that he'd followed his dream and was now a firefighter...maybe it had been for the best that she didn't tell him.

"Look." Andrew leaned in close. "It's not too late. She's only a year and a half. Still a baby. He didn't miss out on anything."

She had to disagree with him there. Jonas had missed out on a lot. Still, she nodded. "I guess."

"Right. If you want to tell him tomorrow, you can finally know for sure what he thinks. If he's a rat bastard, he'll prove you did the right thing. If he wants to be part of Meg's life, then you still did the right thing. The man's a firefighter now, got a good career. He wouldn't have had that if he'd stayed here."

She frowned at that. "Why do I get the feeling you're trying to make this out to be better than it is?"

Andrew shrugged. "Felt bad for giving you that tough love a minute ago. Either way, nothing too important was lost. And everything aside, having him around might be good for you with everything going on. Even a subhuman can keep other males away."

"Jonas hates being called a subhuman."

Andrew grinned at her, knocking his knuckles on the table. "There, you see? Already you're defending him like you used to."

Taylor looked down at Meg, who more and more appeared as though she was not going to resume her nap, which meant she had to get out of here and fast. "I don't want to spring this on him."

Andrew shrugged, as though to ask *what can I do?*

"You might not have much choice on that one. If he's coming around, he's going to see you with her. He's going to do some quick math in his head and figure things out. If you tell him first, it will be better than if he finds out some other way."

Taylor swallowed just as Meg gave out her first hungry cry. She stood.

"I hate it when you're right."

Andrew stood with her, walking her to the door. "Just make sure to keep him away from our business if you do give him the news. If I can get the other packs and skulks to come together with this, then we might finally get some peace and quiet around here."

Taylor nodded. She didn't like it. She didn't want forgiveness for someone who was out there starting fires in the forest area around Lakeview. Someone like that had to be unhinged. She sure as hell wouldn't want that person as a neighbor.

Which was why she thought it might be for the best if Andrew decided to let Jonas, and his boss, in on what was going on around here.

Taylor went to her trailer, fed Meg before putting her into her playpen, then pulled out the card Jonas had left her with when he left the daycare earlier that morning.

She put the card to her nose, inhaling his scent.

When he'd been in front of her, it had been a struggle not to fall into his arms, to let that intoxicating smell get the better of her. Scent was tied to so many of her memories. She'd heard it was this way even with humans, who did not have such a strong sense of smell.

For Taylor, scent was everything. She'd smelled him the moment she'd opened the door and spotted him, and she'd smelled nothing but him after, even when she'd been trying to work.

The only thing of his she had on her now was his child and this card.

Taylor had always thought Meg smelled a little like him, but now she knew that was nothing in comparison to having Jonas right in front of her.

Taylor pulled the card away from her nose, then smiled at her daughter, who looked at her strangely while chewing on one of her toys.

"Momma's weird, right?"

Meg didn't reply.

Taylor reached for her phone. She played with the idea of a text; she thought of it long and hard, how much easier that would be.

Instead, she dialed his number, her heart hammering, and Meg held her breath until he picked up.

"I was hoping you'd call."

His voice, smooth like butter in her ear, had her ensnared already. "I want to see you."

CHAPTER 3

*J*onas tapped his fingers on the small table of the little cafe. Lakeview managed to pull in a couple of extra small businesses since he'd lived here. It stunned him to see some of these places, but the hiking trails, rivers, and mountain views were bound to pull people in who wanted the outdoor experience without paying higher prices to other nature towns.

The coffee here wasn't as expensive as in the city, and not as expensive as a full-blown tourist town, but it was a higher cost than he remembered it being.

He was on his third cup, and damn near jittering out of his seat when he finally allowed himself to check his phone.

Taylor was fifteen minutes late. But she'd always been late, so he'd expected that. But as each minute ticked by, he was more and more convinced that she wasn't just late, that she wasn't going to show up at all.

She kept her daycare open on Saturdays, and he'd wanted to pick her up after work, but he resisted the urge to offer. He didn't want to come off as being too clingy. Too eager. That could scare off even the strongest of women.

And considering how they'd ended things...

Taylor said she wanted to meet him, that she had something to show him. But for the life of him, he couldn't think of anything other than how much he wanted to taste her mouth again. All sorts of needs and desires he'd thought were long dead were alive and roaring again now that he was back in this place.

The waitress returned to him, asked him if he wanted another refill.

He looked at his phone. Twenty-five minutes late. If she really was late and not just ditching him, then this was pushing it even for her.

"I'll take the check, please."

He'd wait another ten minutes after that, and then it would be time for him to go. He pulled out some cash, enough to cover his four dollar coffee and the tip and placed it on the table before leaning back in his chair, trying not to let the disappointment get the best of him too much.

"Goddamnit."

Jonas was getting ready to leave when he spotted her, her shiny, black head of hair gleaming in the sunlight just through the windows of the cafe as she rushed down the sidewalk and through the glass doors.

Jonas paused. Relief. He shouldn't feel this kind of emotion when it came to her, but he couldn't help himself either.

He was relieved she was here. So much that it stunned him.

Taylor spotted him just as the waitress came to her. Taylor pointed, indicating she was meeting up with him, then made her way to his table, pulling off the summer jacket she wore.

"Sorry I'm late. One of the parents kept telling me another five minutes, and they were going to be here."

He nodded. He didn't point out that she could have texted him that, knowing how she was with answering any of her messages, and he didn't want to start this off on a fight.

"I was starting to worry you weren't just a little late."

She smiled, as though remembering old times. Or was that just what he was thinking?

"Sorry." Taylor still smiled at him, and there was something...almost scared in that. It got his protective instincts up and roaring in an instant.

Later. If this were what he thought it was, he would deal with that later.

"How've you been?"

Taylor cleared her throat. "Good. Yeah, everything's been real good."

He could tell she was lying. Everything wasn't good.

They used to play a game together. Taylor would tell him something blatantly false, and he would determine whether or not she was lying. About ninety percent of the time, he was always on point. There was the odd time when she could get one over him, but it was so rare that he was confident he could read her like a book.

Now was one of those times. Of course, she could just be trying to make friendly conversation. Everyone made nice conversation even when they were having a shit day.

"Are you ready to tell me what's going on with the fires?"

Taylor sucked back a breath, her spine going straight.

He backed off a little. "You don't have to get into specifics, and you don't even have to give me a name if you don't have it, but anything at all; you can be completely anonymous if you're worried about what the pack will think."

"You know it's not as simple as that. Everyone always finds out something about everyone else around here. If I say anything, it will get back to the people responsible."

His captain would love to hear that confirmed. That there actually was someone responsible for this.

"Is it someone, or someones, who are responsible?"

"Jonas, that's not..." She sighed, and he could tell this wasn't something she wanted to get in to.

That was just too damned bad for her. He was going to get it out of her, even if he had to play this long, slow game.

He leaned across the table, which was relatively easy considering how small it was and that his entire upper body took up most of the space.

"I know how things work. I get it, you don't want to rat anyone out, but this is serious—"

"I am being serious." She glanced around, as though making sure no one with prominent ears or tails could hear them.

Jonas had spotted no shifters, but she still acted as though the walls had ears as she leaned in close. "You know how things work around here. It's not a matter of not wanting to tell who's doing what. It's that I can't. You know that."

She tapped her finger hard onto the table, as though to accent her point.

The worst part was that he did know. It was the reason why he'd wanted to leave. Why he'd gotten so sick of the whole shifter community, he'd wanted to go and take Taylor with him.

But she didn't want to go. She wanted to stay, and she didn't want to be with a man who couldn't shift.

Now, he was getting pissed off. He didn't want that. If he didn't pull that shit back, she was going to sense it, and he was going to get nowhere.

Jonas took in a deep breath. "People could get hurt. People's lives could be ruined."

"And my sloth could get hurt. My—" she paused, seemed to collect herself, then continued. "Shifters don't like bringing humans into their business. I tried talking with Andrew, pointing out that you're not entirely..."

He tried not to grit his teeth together too much. "Human?"

Taylor briefly pressed her lips together. "Yeah. It wasn't enough."

He hated that. He fucking hated how it was such a big deal to the shifters when one of their own turned out to be a subhuman. Born to shifters, but couldn't shift. It led to a mother who always looked at him as though he was the reason his father had left and a perfect romance that dissolved when Taylor couldn't see past it either.

He hated shifters sometimes, he really did.

"You work with children. Toddlers and babies. If one of them got hurt, or worse, because of one of these fires, and you didn't tell me anything when you had the chance, would you feel guilty about that? Or would you be all right with yourself?"

Taylor jerked back, wide eyes blinking, as though he'd just physically assaulted her. "What?"

He shrugged, leaning back in his seat. "It's an honest question. I'm trying to find out who is starting these fires. At this point, I don't even care about why. But the sooner you give that information to me, or the police, the better. Don't give me the name if you don't trust me. Make an anonymous call to the police. You're allowed to do that. But if one of those babies is hurt because of this, it will be on you."

Taylor shook her head. "You can't put that on me."

"I can, and I am. It's on everyone here who knows and is too stubborn to let a bunch of filthy humans in on their business."

Taylor narrowed her eyes, getting angry. Good. He wanted her angry. "Jesus, Jonas, I know you left and everything, but you do remember that packs don't take kindly to shifters who bring humans into their affairs, right?"

"So what? I can protect you."

She jerked back again. "What?"

He hadn't meant to say that. Not really, but it was out there now, and he wasn't going to take it back. Jonas leaned forward, his forearms taking up almost all the space on the little round table. "Come with me. I can keep you safe. You don't have to live under people you're afraid of. You don't need a pack."

She stared at him as though he was speaking in tongues. "You're the one who doesn't like shifters."

"I don't like shifters, but I like you."

Always had. In fact, the L word he wanted to use for her was a little stronger than like.

"I am a shifter."

Jonas leaned back in his seat, sighing.

Taylor looked at him, as though waiting for him to say anything else.

When he didn't have anything for her, she shook her head and crossed her arms.

Jonas frowned. "Wait, did you leave me because you thought I wouldn't want you as a shifter?" Taylor said nothing to that. She barely glanced at him, but it was enough for him to get the message straight. "Jesus Christ, are you serious? You broke up with me because you thought I wouldn't want to be with you? Where the hell would you get an idea like that?"

He shouldn't be angry. It was over. It was years ago. Jonas thought he'd buried the need to know, the need for closure. He should be doing so many things other than rehashing an old relationship, but now that it was here within his grasp, he found himself needing to know.

"You were the one who always said you couldn't wait to get out of here."

"Right, because the shifters here kept looking at me like I was dirt. You knew that. I told you literally everything about me." And he did mean everything. She knew what his home life was like. She knew what his mother thought of him.

Hell, the one time he'd brought her over for dinner, he'd heard his mom asking Taylor if she was all right with the idea of dating a subhuman. Someone who might not be able to give her shifter children.

He'd pretended not to hear that shit, but he hadn't brought Taylor over again.

Then, she broke his damn heart.

"You're the one who didn't want to be with a subhuman."

Her eyes popped wide. "I never said that!"

He reached for his nearly empty coffee mug. "Yes, you did."

Taylor shook her head. "I'm telling you, I didn't say that! I wouldn't say that!"

"Why are you arguing with me about this? I know what I heard."

"I wouldn't say that to you!" Taylor snapped her lips shut, once more glancing around the cafe, and this time, there were a couple of patrons who were looking over at them, as though wondering what the matter was.

Taylor lifted her hands, elbows on the table, as though trying to hide her face.

Jonas wasn't ashamed. He didn't care who heard him. He should care, but he didn't.

"I promise, I didn't say that, Jonas. Maybe you thought you heard it because of...how difficult it was."

"Right, it was just in my head that my girlfriend wanted to leave me because I was a subhuman."

She glared back at him. "Uh huh, and was it in my head every time you complained to me about how terrible shifters were? How we were all tribal and ignorant and cruel?"

"I was never talking about you, and you know it." That she could make his pain out to be about her was seriously making him question why he still had a candle lit for her at all. "It wasn't just that, I was...Goddamnit, you have no idea what I was going through, okay?"

She stared at him, and when he noted the misty shine in her eyes, Jonas's gut tightened.

"I didn't just...I loved you, all right? You knew that it was never something fake for me. But you only wanted me around because being with a shifter made you look better to the elders. You can't put all this on me and pretend you weren't using me to up your status because that's exactly what you were doing. I knew it, and I still loved you, you asshole."

She wasn't yelling this time, but Taylor still glanced around to make sure no one was listening to their conversation.

Of course, someone would be. Even humans could pick up on the fact that something was going on.

And Jonas shook his head. "That was never why I was with you."

Taylor looked at him, her eyes doe-like, and she rubbed at them, grabbing her jacket and standing. "Screw you."

"What?"

She marched to the door. Jonas went after her.

No way. No fucking way was he letting her walk out on him again after dropping something like that.

He rushed out onto the sidewalk after her. "Hey, will you stop for two minutes? Where the hell did you get the idea that I was only with you to look good? What about me hating the elders and the shifter hierarchy made you think I only wanted you for...for that?"

He could hardly put it into words. It was so ridiculously stupid he wanted to yank all of his hair out.

"Go away!"

Her car was parked on the side of the road down the street. She pulled out her keys and unlocked her car door before making it to the vehicle. When she did, Jonas had to hurry. He slammed his palm onto the glass, shutting the door when she tried to open it.

Taylor wet her lips, still refusing to look at him, but he could see the tears in her eyes. "Leave me alone, please."

"No way. You seriously think I was using you? What part of I love you, Taylor, made you think that?"

She wiped at her eyes, took in a breath, and he saw something like shame in her expression that made him understand.

"Was it Andrew who told you that? Or your elders?"

"I went to them for advice when you said you wanted to leave. And for...something else."

"Something else? Are you serious right now?"

She glared at him, and he realized he was probably being too rough.

Jonas took his hand off the car door. She didn't open it right away. She just stared at him.

"You didn't like shifters; that's exactly what I was, and you weren't going to stay. It was never about you being a subhuman to me, not ever."

"Well, I never hated you for being a shifter and never used you to look good to any pack."

"So what? We're both wrong?"

He didn't want to be wrong. He wanted to be right. He wanted to be right and make her apologize. But he wasn't going to get that, and part of him knew deep down that, as much as he wanted to be the one who was wholly inno-cent, he wasn't.

"I think we both misunderstood some things, and I don't think your elders helped anything out by giving bad advice."

Taylor inhaled deeply, letting it out slowly. "I went to see them because I was pregnant, Jonas. And I didn't know what to do."

He blinked. He was waiting for his brain to turn those sounds into something other than what he'd just heard.

Getting kicked in the nuts would have felt better than this.

CHAPTER 4

Taylor didn't like Jonas' reaction. The way he stared at her, as though demanding to know if what she was saying happened to be a nasty joke of some kind...

She wasn't joking, and she could have told him much easier than that.

Now they were standing here between the cafe and the local laundromat, and Taylor started wishing a fire would start up right now so she could have an excuse to be somewhere else.

Of course, she wasn't sure what Jonas' responsibilities would be if a fire occurred in a tiny town where he didn't work or live.

And he was still staring at her.

"You want to say that to me again?"

His voice was low, dangerous. Even a little scared.

"I was pregnant." She opened her mouth to say something else. Anything else, but nothing would come out other than the most useless words there were. "I'm sorry."

Jonas' spine stiffened. He stepped away from her, rubbing his jaw, his other hand on his waist as he paced the alley.

Occasionally, he would look up at her, his expression one she couldn't read. Taylor had never felt more like a jerk in her entire life than she did at that moment.

When Jonas finally spoke up, she was grateful to hear something other than her own terrified inner screams. "You said were. Past tense. Okay, obviously, that was a while ago. Did…did you keep it?"

"I did."

His eyes flared up. "And you never told me about this?"

"It wasn't…it wasn't like that."

"Jesus Christ, Taylor, what was it like? You're telling me I'm a father?" Something seemed to hit him just then. "One of those kids in that room. One of them was mine."

She nodded. "Yeah."

"That's why you started the daycare."

She nodded again. "Yes."

He looked away from her, shaking his head, his mouth and jaw tightening. "You…fucking bitch."

Taylor cringed.

"Why? What did I ever do to you? I wasn't some abusive prick. I wouldn't have pressured you to get rid of it. I wouldn't have walked out on you. You didn't have any reason to hide it from me or send me away."

She didn't have an answer, which meant Jonas came up with his own.

"Right. You didn't want some subhuman raising your kid, is that it?"

"No!"

He didn't believe her. "Then what? Tell me why you did this to me!"

"I didn't do it to you! It wasn't supposed to be like that! I just…I thought you didn't want anything to do with shifters. I thought you wouldn't want to have a baby with me if you knew, and then you wanted to leave, and I didn't…"

He shook his head. "You should have told me. You had no right to keep something like that from me."

"I know. I meant to tell you after I gave birth, but then I was feeding a small baby, recovering. I wanted to tell you when I could walk again, but by then it was months later, and it felt like it was too late."

He frowned. "You couldn't walk after?"

The sudden shift in his tone shocked her, throwing her off.

"It was…it was a birth. I just needed some time."

"Shifters are supposed to heal faster than humans."

"It was a long labor. I'm fine now. I am, so is Meg."

"Meg." He said the word as though it amazed him. "We have a daughter?"

Taylor smiled. "Yeah, we do. She's beautiful. She looks just like you."

"Show me."

Taylor pulled out her phone, scrolled through some photos. She had lots of pictures of her daughter, but at that moment, she wanted to show off only the best ones to Jonas. She wanted to show him exactly how beautiful their daughter was.

She held the phone up. His hand touched hers, steadying the screen, and he groaned.

"She is pretty."

Taylor nodded, her throat closing as Jonas scrolled through the photos. "She is."

He was going through her older catalog now. She could see herself in some of those pictures. She was exhausted, in bed, holding her tiny daughter, breast-feeding hours after Meg finally deemed it right to come into the world.

"How long were you in labor for?"

Taylor didn't want to say, because she knew it would make him mad. "Almost twenty-four hours."

She'd been right. He was mad. She could see it in his eyes.

"I'm fine."

"I'm trained in first aid; I know that's wading into dangerous territory."

"I know, and Andrew promised to bring me to a hospital for a C-section if it lasted any longer."

"You gave birth at home?"

She grit her teeth. "Shifters do it all the time. It's easier for me to smell familiar things. People. No chemicals."

"Taylor, this is why you can't always do what your pack tells you to. You should have been in a hospital. What if you'd died?"

"That wasn't going to happen because Andrew and the elders were there to take care of us. He promised me he would call for an ambulance if it lasted any longer. He said he would drive me to the hospital himself if it looked dangerous."

The problem was how he didn't look as though he believed her.

"I'm telling you the truth!"

"It's not you I don't believe." He shoved her phone back at her. "When can I see her?"

Taylor pressed her lips together. "I brought her to a sitter before coming to see you. You can come with me to pick her up if you like."

"Who's watching her?"

"Andrew is."

Jonas nodded. Taylor expected him to get angry again, to demand to know why she hadn't brought Meg with her, why she'd left their daughter in the care of her alpha, but he didn't say any of those things.

"All right. Let's go."

She blinked. "You want to come?"

He pulled his keys from his jacket pocket. "Of course I do. I want to meet my kid."

Taylor thought he wouldn't want to be anywhere near her sloth, but she supposed she'd underestimated how much this would affect him.

And she felt like a jerk all over again just for that.

"Right, uh, do want to drive with me?"

Jonas shook his head. "No, I've got my own ride. I'll follow you."

The chill in his voice made her shiver.

She'd never heard him speak like this to her before, and it did something to her. Something deep inside.

It made her want to shrivel up and vanish into a dark hole.

Jonas hated her, and she couldn't blame him for it.

"Are we going?"

Taylor nodded, sucking it up.

She had her daughter to think about, and what she was going to do about the other reason why Jonas was here.

"Okay, I'm parked out back, don't drive off without me."

"Do you really think I would?"

He looked at her, but he didn't answer.

She tried not to cringe.

This was going to be tough.

* * *

THEY MADE it back to her territory in decent time. Taylor tried not to look at the charred trees on the ride home, and decided not to think of the words Jonas had said to her back at the cafe. She wasn't going to let anything happen to Meg. She could swear on her life to that. Things were going to be all right, and now that she was bringing Jonas to her territory, maybe he could make his case to Andrew.

They parked in front of her trailer. A few of the parents and cubs looked her way when a truck that was newer, nicer, and had no rust on it parked next to her old Nissan. It didn't look as though it fit the scene, but it didn't matter to her right then.

These people might recognize Jonas, or not. It wasn't any of her concern. She was facing a more important event than her neighbors could imagine.

"This is where you live?"

Taylor had to catch herself before she could glare at him. "This is indeed where I live."

Jonas looked it over. She got the feeling he was silently judging her, and she hated that.

This hadn't been his sloth. Jonas had been born to bear shifters, but they weren't part of her territory.

Not officially.

He'd lived nearby, his mother trying to get into the clan, but she had little to offer, no mate, and her son was a subhuman.

At the time, Taylor had wondered why she didn't just take her son to the city to live with the humans, but as she and Jonas became friends, that became more of a fear as she got older. She hadn't wanted her best friend taken to live with the humans. She'd wanted Jonas to live here with her as an official member of their group.

As they got older, and even as they started dating, she'd realized more and more how that was never going to happen. He resented the way others looked at him for not having his ears and tail, for being unable to shift.

Looking at him now, as Jonas glanced around at the other trailers on the territory, at the people and cubs he'd never met before, she wondered if living with the humans had treated him as well as he'd always hoped.

Some humans loved the idea of subhumans. People with higher than average strength, speed, and recovery time. Other humans, from what Taylor read on the Internet, were as nervous around subhumans as they were around the shifters.

It was as though the subhumans couldn't win no matter how hard they tried.

"That house over there, is it new?"

Taylor nodded. "Yeah, construction started shortly after you left. The elders live there."

He smirked. "So, kind of an old age home for the gossip mongers, eh?"

"What?" Taylor had to stuff her hand over her face to

cover the snort that threatened to come out. "Don't say that!"

He shrugged, his grin showing off the whites of his teeth. "Why not? Not like it isn't true? Elders are only useful for giving out terrible advice and pretending to be wise and knowledgeable."

"They are. They're older. They have more experience." Even as she said it, Taylor still struggled not to laugh.

And the way Jonas smiled made it so easy for her to relax. He wasn't giving off the angry vibe from earlier. She couldn't feel anger and heat radiating from him anymore, and it felt nice to act like they used to around each other.

"Experience in what, exactly? Nagging at everyone under a hundred they can get their hands on? Honestly, I don't know why packs have them around anymore. If you want family advice, some therapists are specifically trained for that sort of thing. Degrees and everything."

"Someone's going to hear you talking like that, and you're going to get us in trouble."

He shrugged. "Well, you might get in trouble. I won't."

She shoved him on the arm as they headed to Andrew's small house. "You'll still get in trouble."

"If I don't care that I'm in trouble from a bunch of do-gooder elders, and I don't have to live here, does it still count?"

She knocked on Andrew's door. "That sounds like a tree falling in the woods and making a sound type of question."

"It is, but this one has an answer."

She groaned, wishing he didn't look so good with that stupid smile on his face.

Elders weren't as common as they used to be, and if she was honest with herself, Taylor was grateful for that because she didn't much like the elders either.

Still, she wasn't about to openly insult them when anyone could hear. Hell, the elders themselves might have listened to those comments if they only had their windows open to listen.

Her small ears perked as she heard the footsteps inside. Andrew unlocked his door, opened wide, but he didn't smile.

Because he could clearly see Jonas standing next to her.

"So you've made your decision?"

Any mirth she'd felt after Jonas' teasing left her in a mere instant, and just like that, she was back to this dark place again. "Yeah. Was Meg good for you today?"

"Like an angel after I put on some Shimmer and Shine videos. I think I hate that show now."

Taylor smiled. Jonas frowned. "What's Shimmer and Shine?"

Something long, sharp, and merciless pierced her heart at that.

Jonas didn't know the basics of what her little girl liked to watch. He didn't know what these animated characters were, because she'd denied him that.

"I'll show you, come on."

It wasn't lost on her the way Andrew eyeballed Jonas as the other man stepped into his home. She also noticed that Jonas didn't follow her lead and take off his shoes, though she supposed he wasn't in a mood to convey any respect to Andrew as they headed through his house.

Taylor let Jonas take the lead and followed close

behind him. She wanted to keep him within her sights. Wanted to see his face when he saw his daughter. She couldn't even explain why that was.

He came to a dead stop in the entryway to the sitting room. Taylor stopped just behind him, and it was easy to see what had caught his attention.

Her throat closed. Meg was in her playpen, sitting up, her favorite teddy bear gripped tightly in her little arms while she looked up at the bright colors playing out on Andrew's forty-inch flat screen.

Taylor heard a soft, choked noise leave Jonas' throat as Meg turned to look at him, and felt everything around her play out in slow motion after that.

CHAPTER 5

His own eyes looked up at him, from the tiny frame of a little girl set up comfortably inside a children's playpen, surrounded by colorful toys. The cogs in his brain struggled to try to process what he was seeing, to make him believe that this tiny person he hadn't known existed a mere hour ago was actually here.

He kept waiting for her to disappear, for him to come to his senses. It couldn't be real. How could it be real when this morning it hadn't been?

He stepped into the sitting room, aware of the light creaking noise coming from the floorboards beneath his weight. As he approached, the little girl did not vanish, as a figment of his imagination would. Instead, she smiled up at him, and his heart did something it had never done before. Something twisty and painful.

Something on the edge of terror and elation.

Because this was his, he'd made this. Helped make it, really. She was a piece of him.

As he got closer, Jonas was able to take in more details.

The little yellow dress she wore, the way her dark curls floofed out on top of her head, and the way she still smiled up at him. It all made no sense. She didn't know him. Was it because Taylor was in the room with him? Her mother around would make this stranger in front of her easier to handle, he supposed.

But the girl, Meg, didn't look to Taylor. She kept looking right at him. Chubby fists were squeezing around the leg of her bear. She lifted it again and again, making unintelligible noises.

He reached his hand down into the playpen, and she reached the bear up, seeming to toss it into his hand.

"I think she wants to share it with you."

Jonas blinked and turned his attention to the spot beside him. He'd been so stuck with this tunnel vision of his daughter that he hadn't noticed when Taylor came to stand right beside him.

Taylor smiled at him. She seemed to be suffering from a similar fear of his own, but he realized it wasn't a fear brought on from realizing she was a parent out of the blue. It was a fear of what his reaction would be.

Jonas swallowed, struggling to keep control over the sound of his erratically beating heart. He took the bear, looked at it, then back down at Meg. "Thanks."

She gurgled, then finally seemed to notice her mother before raising her arms.

Taylor complied, reached in, and pulled Meg out, settling the child with an evident familiarity against her chest. As though she'd held her daughter like that a thousand times before.

Right. So dumb. She had held Meg like that a thousand times before. This ease with which she carried her daughter had nothing to do with her experience running a daycare. This was instinct.

"Hello, baby. Were you a good girl today?"

Meg responded in a string of babbles that sounded like "mama," and emphasized her chatter with harmless fists on her mother's chest, as though trying to beat on a drum while grinning up at Taylor.

Jonas couldn't seem to get his breath.

Part of him thought he should have known. He wasn't a shifter, but he was part shifter. His parents were shifters. Subhumans still had some level of strength. Higher than average muscle mass, stronger bone density, and even a slight advantage to healing time when it came to wounds and the common cold.

He should have known. Something instinctual should have alerted him that there was a tiny person out there in the world who had his blood, who looked like him, who had his eyes, who lived and breathed...he should have known.

Part of him wanted to go back to being angry with Taylor. He was still mad at her. He was pissed off beyond all reason, and yet he couldn't bring himself to do that.

The sight in front of him was too...awe inspiring.

Taylor smiled at the little girl in her arms. Did she know she was bouncing on her heels as she held the baby like that? Was that a parent thing? Would he have to carry Meg like that to keep her smiling for him?

He didn't think he would mind it if that's what needed to be done to keep the little girl gurgling and grinning like that.

Then Taylor looked at him, and her smile melted away.

He'd never seen Taylor so vulnerable before. In all the years he'd known her, she'd never looked so stark scared while looking at him.

As though waiting for the axe to come down on her neck.

"Do you want to hold her?"

Jonas tensed. His hands gripped the stuffed bear hard enough to strangle it, had it been real, and he didn't trust himself to put a fragile baby in his arms.

"Uh, maybe later."

Was that disappointment he saw? Was he imagining that, or...

As Taylor's ears twitched, Jonas noticed for the first time that Meg had little bear ears as well, on either side of her head.

She had human ears as well. Many shifters had both. Some did not, but he noted the way her hair was styled to cover her human ears.

Some shifters, the purists, didn't like the human ears. He imagined Taylor didn't want to start any fights with those in her sloth who didn't want to see them on a little shifter girl.

Meg's hair was so curly that he almost hadn't noticed the bear ears anyway.

"She's got the ears. Does she have a tail?"

Taylor smiled, still looking as nervous as could be. "Yeah, she's got a little poof ball." She turned Meg around and revealed the little brown ball of fuzz.

Jonas glanced behind him to Andrew, to make sure he wasn't going insane, and was disappointed to note the alpha was chuckling at him. He responded with a glare.

"Do you want to be in Meg's life?" Taylor's question

pulled his attention back to her. The tone of her voice was serious, but the light in her eyes suggested she knew what the answer would be.

"Y-yeah, of course. I want to...if you're serious, and she's mine. Definitely. I want to be in her life."

And he wanted to catch up on every little thing he'd missed.

"Let's start with holding. Do you want to do that?"

He felt himself gripping the bear again.

Taylor had framed that as a question, but he got the feeling there was only one answer she would accept.

He swallowed hard, set the bear aside, and braced himself. "All right. Sure." He held out his arms. Were his fingers shaking? No, that was in his head.

Taylor looked at his hands, then at him. "She's not made of glass, Jonas."

He clenched his jaw. "I know that!"

Taylor shrugged, then handed the child over a little too quickly for his liking.

Then Meg was in his arms. His little girl. A delicate tiny person. Would she be badly hurt if he dropped her? What if he was too rough? She weighed a little more than he thought, but now Jonas was stuck trying not to grip her too tightly, but still keeping a firm enough hold on her that he didn't drop her.

"You can put her against your chest if you want. It's easier than holding her away from your body like that."

Jonas nodded, his arms already trembling a little from the awkward stance he kept. "Right. I knew that." He pulled Meg to his chest, and he had to admit, it was easier on his arms than what he'd been doing before. He felt as though he could relax somewhat while holding her like this.

Meg chewed on her fist. She looked up at Jonas with wide, innocent brown eyes, and that melting feeling came back to him.

He swallowed hard. "How...how old is she?"

Taylor stood close, watching him, but she also seemed to be enjoying the view. Like a prideful mother.

"A year and six months. Almost seven months."

Jonas counted down the months. That meant she would have been born when there was still snow on the ground — made sense, considering the time when he'd left.

It also meant Taylor had been a couple of months into her pregnancy when she'd broken things off with him. How long had she known?

He didn't ask. Not while he held onto his child. He didn't want to spoil the mood. His daughter was a shifter. Would she be able to sense it if he became upset while holding her? Even human babies were strangely capable of detecting the frequency in the air when it came to the moods of their parents.

Parents.

He was going to have to get used to that.

"I think I need to sit."

He went to the nearest love seat, plopping himself down, and only then realized how weak his knees were. It was a small miracle that he hadn't dropped his daughter in that state.

God. Everything is so messed up.

Taylor sat next to him. She pressed her lips together,

eyeing both Jonas and her daughter with something akin to shame in her eyes. "I'm sorry I didn't tell you."

Jonas looked at her, then down at his daughter. He didn't answer her. He touched the little bear ears on her head. They were strikingly soft. He'd touched kittens with coarser hair than that.

Taylor took his silence as a negative, pushing forward. "It wasn't that I meant to keep this from you. It was never my...weeks just turned into months, and then the months turned into two years. I started thinking to myself that it was probably for the best that you didn't know, that I didn't tell you. That it was too late, you know?"

Jonas shook his head. "Not really." He glanced at her, noting the flinch.

Maybe Meg really could read the frequency in the air, because immediately after that happened, she reached out to her mother, babbling for "mama," and Jonas had no choice but to hand her over.

Taylor took her daughter, the shamed expression still on her face as she held Meg close, looking very much like a mother bear guarding a treasure.

He needed to extend an olive branch of some kind. "I don't resent you for having her. I'm just pissed off that I didn't know."

Taylor nodded. "Yeah, I know."

Much as he was looking for a fight with her at the cafe earlier, now knew he wasn't going to get anywhere that way. Looking at Taylor holding his child filled him with mixed emotions. The anger at not knowing was there, but also, strangely enough, something not-so-angry too...

Almost protective. That was the word he was looking for.

Which was kind of stupid because it meant he wanted to protect this woman and little girl from, essentially, himself.

Jonas sighed. "You said it was the elders who convinced you to break things off?"

Taylor looked at him, then stroked Meg's hair. "That's not an excuse. I should have known well enough to make up my mind."

"That's not what I asked. You went for their advice, and they told you to ditch me?"

Taylor pressed her lips together. "Not quite like that, but...ugh, it just makes me so mad to think about it! If I hadn't been so stupid about it, Meg would know you. She wouldn't be looking at you right now like you're a stranger!"

He hadn't realized she looked at him like that, but he also had no idea what any baby look might mean.

"I talked with Andrew yesterday, just after you came to visit the daycare," Taylor started. "I wanted to blame the elders, too. They didn't want me to date you. They worried if we...did anything, that any kids we had would be...you know."

"Subhumans?"

She flinched. "I know you don't like that word."

"Still don't, but...there's no point in getting around it. And, ultimately, I know you don't mean it like they do anyway. I know you're not trying to hurt me, so there's no point in getting mad about it."

Taylor still appeared uncomfortable, but she continued. "Well, they worried that Meg wouldn't be able to shift. They advised me to..." She hesitated, then actually pressed her hands over both sets of Meg's ears. With Meg's size, it was doable. "Terminate the pregnancy."

Jonas felt a familiar spark of anger well up within him at the thought that Meg would not exist if the elders had their way...and it would have been for nothing, too. She was clearly a little shifter. She was everything they wanted her to be, but because of what her father was, there was still the stigma.

Jonas never thought he would see shifters stuck with that same stigma as the subhumans. It seemed so utterly unfair. So backward.

"Why didn't you? You got me to leave. One of the three times in our lives together you tricked me into believing something you'd said even though it wasn't true. I would never have known, and no one here would have judged you for it."

Taylor swallowed, inhaling a deep breath through her nose. "I couldn't do it. Every day that went by she became more and more real. I just couldn't go through with it. I thought of calling you, but I worried you wouldn't take my calls, then I was scared you wouldn't want to come anyway. I didn't know whether to hope she would be a human or a shifter. If she were a human, the pack would treat her badly, but if she was a shifter, which she turned out to be..."

"You thought I wouldn't want her?"

Again, he could tell when Taylor bit the inside of her cheek. "Part of me hoped it wouldn't matter, but again, the days just kept going by, and telling you seemed more and more like something that would never happen as each day went by. I'm sorry, I know that doesn't make any sense."

She looked at him, then glanced away again.

That fragile aura around her wasn't right. He couldn't stand that in her. She was so much stronger than that. She deserved so much better. There was no reason for her to be cowed down to him or anyone else.

"I'm still angry, but the more you tell me, the more I'm not angry at you."

"But you're still angry."

"Yeah, at the elders who gave you their horseshi—uh, their garbage advice. At Andrew for not talking you out of it, and everyone else in this sloth for making you think if you had a subhuman baby that you'd both be lesser for it. It's all a bunch of crap. I'm not mad at you. I'm mad at all of them, and the sloth culture that put you in an impossible situation."

He looked at her, right in her eyes, and he felt a little ashamed of himself. "I'm sorry I called you a bitch."

She smiled softly at him. Almost shyly. And she was so damned beautiful he couldn't stand it.

"It's fine. I get it."

"It's not fine."

"Jonas, I promise. I'm fine."

She looked like she meant it, but he didn't want to leave it like this. He didn't want her to think he hated her.

Before he could get another word out, Jonas heard a commotion outside. Nothing sharp or heavy, but he'd worked with the public long enough to recognize the feel in the air when people were gathering around, shouting at each other, with a touch of panic in their tones.

Taylor's ears twitched. Of course, she heard it, too. Her sense of hearing was better than his. "What's going on?"

He shook his head. "Not sure."

Andrew's heavy boots stomped through the house,

down the hall, and to the front door. Jonas and Taylor looked at each other before following him.

Jonas rushed a little faster after the alpha. "Andrew, what's going on?"

"Hell if I know," he replied, pushing his way out the door, Jonas on his heels.

The first thing he noted was the way the sloth gathered around. They were in front of Andrew's house, but not facing it. Not facing each other or the ground either, which would have been the case if they were watching a fight.

No. They stared up the mountain, at the forest that covered it, and as his gaze followed their direction, his nose caught the scent in the air of burning.

A heavy rumble in the sky announced a plane flying overhead towards the pillar of smoke snaking towards the sky.

A pillar that wasn't so far away either.

"Oh my God." Jonas glanced to the side at Taylor's whispered fears. She still had Meg in her arms, the little girl completely unaware of what was going on around her.

Yeah. It was way too close.

CHAPTER 6

"Will we have to leave?"

Taylor saw a familiar look in Jonas' eyes when looked at her. Something urgent, even a little dangerous.

He wanted to go up there. He wanted to be with the plane that was currently dropping water and retardant onto the fire below the cloud of smoke. Ever since they were kids, he'd wanted a job where he could protect and care for people. Now that he had it, Taylor found herself fearful.

For him.

"Probably not, but just to be safe, go make sure you have some essentials packed up. It's better to head out and come back in a bit than to try to wait it out and end up trapped."

Taylor nodded. This fire wasn't as close as the last one, but it was still too close for her comfort.

Andrew was trying to get his people moving, to get them to stop watching the fire and go gather their cubs, but it wasn't until Jonas stepped up beside him that Taylor noticed a change. He drew their attention with a clap of his hands and the boom of his voice. "Okay, listen up. My name is Jonas MacBride, some of you may recognize me. I'm a Lieutenant with the Astraea Fire Department just outside of Washington. Andrew called me in to help keep things as calm and collected as possible in the event of a situation such as this. Everyone who has an emergency bag packed with at least three days' worth of food, water, clothes, and other necessities, raise your hand, please."

Taylor had some things packed away in case she needed to make a hasty exit, but it was not three days' worth. It turned out the majority of her sloth was in a similar boat to her because it looked as though less than ten people raised their hands. Even Andrew didn't.

Jonas nodded. "All right. Those of you who do not have these provisions packed away, go to your homes, grab a gym bag, or your backpacks, whatever you have, and get these things together. Anyone who has battery-powered radios, or First Aid kits, add those to your packs as well."

"Are we leaving?" someone asked, echoing the same question Taylor asked a moment before.

Jonas looked back to the plane circling the pillar of smoke before glancing at her. "That is unlikely for now, but Andrew and I want to make sure you are all prepared for the event of an emergency. Keep your radios on; if there is to be an evacuation, they'll broadcast it to us. Go and pack. Listen to your radios. I will come around to make sure each and every one of you has something of use in your bags. If you have any questions, I will answer them."

People started going back to their homes almost immediately after Jonas stopped talking. He only had to reiterate once that he needed them to start moving and to go right away.

He hid it well, but Taylor could see a level of shock on his face. Was he that surprised that the people were listening to him? He hadn't gotten much respect as a subhuman, but he'd stood tall and showed himself to be a man of authority in an emergency. Even shifters would respond to that sort of behavior.

Andrew slapped Jonas on the back, pulling him out of the trance he'd fallen into.

Andrew laughed. "Good work. Didn't expect that out of you."

"Yeah," Jonas said softly.

Had he not expected it either?

Jonas quickly returned to her side. "Do you have anything packed up?"

"I've got a day bag for her and a first aid kit."

She knew that wasn't enough even before he pointed it out.

"All right. We're going to have to work with a little more than that. Come on; I'll help you out." He took her by the arm. His grip was firm but gentle.

She couldn't describe how it felt. He wanted her to move, but she wasn't getting the feeling that he was in a panic. She felt it in his aura. He knew what he was doing. He could help her get what she needed going, and the air about him wasn't spreading any fear. In fact, his touch calmed her. She could see he was very good at his job. The people he helped were better for having him around.

At her house, he opened the door for her, then stepped aside so she could enter with Meg first.

"Where's your First Aid kit?"

"Under the kitchen sink." She pointed to it, though it was readily observable, connected to her living room in the open-concept floorplan.

He moved to the sink, quick, but again, not giving off any vibes that this was a red line kind of emergency.

"Are you sure we won't have to leave?"

He pulled the kit up and onto the counter. It was one of the bigger ones she'd purchased after the last fire made it a little too close to the territory. On sale. She hoped everything inside it would be to Jonas' standards as he opened it and had a look through.

"No way to know for sure, but it's better to be prepared. This is a good one. You got a radio around here?"

She thought about it. "The stereo over there." She pointed to the spot beside her TV. It was an older CD player with a radio attachment. She'd picked it up on sale as well for about twenty dollars. It was not the sort of thing she could take with her. For one thing, it didn't run on batteries, and it needed to be plugged into the wall. Not exactly the sort of thing a person used in an emergency.

Jonas took note of that. "Yeah, you're going to need something a little more portable."

"If we get into a car, would we really need a battery operated radio?" She felt kind of stupid for asking even as she packed extra diapers into Meg's day bag. Meg sat on the floor, a reminder that even though Jonas seemed calm and business-like, there was a real potential danger in the area that could put their lives at stake.

"We won't always be in a vehicle, and when you're on the run, you don't ever want to keep your gas running, or the car battery turned on. You need to save up as much power as possible." He stopped surveying the living room, as though searching for anything else that could be of use to her. "If you don't have one, someone else will, and if your sloth leaves they'll at least travel together. So we won't worry about that one. Is that where you keep all your canned goods?"

She nodded. "I've got another bag in my closet. Can you watch her?"

"Of course."

How was he so calm? She didn't understand it but knew he had to be trained for this sort of situation, and even if there were some part of him that was in the middle of a mild panic attack, he would know how to hide that from her so well that she wouldn't be able to sense it.

Taylor's hands trembled as she yanked out her gym bag from the back of her closet. She turned it upside down, dumping her yoga gear out and going to her dresser. She put spare clothes for herself inside and then filled it with clothes for Meg. Little socks, dresses. She grabbed all the essentials she could get her hands on that were around her dresser. Wipes for Meg, some extra cash she had lying there, that pack of batteries for her flash-light that suddenly seemed much more critical than usual.

She rushed into her bathroom next, grabbing her toothbrush, Meg's baby shampoo. There were so many other things she was pretty sure she was forgetting, and yet she couldn't bring herself to remember everything.

She had to remember to keep room for bottled water and soup cans.

"Hey."

Taylor jumped, her heart hurtling into her throat. "Jesus, you scared me."

Jonas stood in the doorway, holding Meg in his arms. He looked so natural like that, even though he'd just found out he was a father.

"You can relax. The radio isn't calling for an evacuation."

She nodded. "I know, you said they said that probably wasn't going to happen, but I just figured...isn't it a bad thing that I wasn't ready anyway? Shouldn't I have been ready?"

He smiled at her, though there was nothing unkind in it. "The vast majority of people are supposed to have emergency supplies put away in their homes and cars, and almost no one has those things prepared. You've got a First Aid kit in your house. That's so much more than what I see so many people doing for their families. Try not to worry about it."

Taylor pressed her lips together. Her eyes stung, and even though he was giving her an out, even though he was being so good about it when he didn't need to be, she felt awful.

She felt like the worst thing in the world she could be — a bad mother.

Jonas stepped into her bathroom. "Hey, you want to tell me what's going on?"

She didn't want to tell him what was going on, because compared to what might be happening outside, the other people who would need him to help with their emergency packs, what she was feeling was nothing.

"Taylor, come on. You can talk to me. Right?"

She inhaled a sharp breath, rubbed at her eyes even though she hadn't spilled any tears.

Yet.

"I just...I hate that this happened. I feel like such a bad mother. I'm not prepared to leave here in a hurry if anything happens. I never told you about Meg, and now these fires are happening, and I'm driving to and from work every day looking at what they did, and I know I should have left. I know all of that, yet I didn't act. Doesn't that make me a bad mother?"

He looked at her, as though searching deep inside her.

"No, it doesn't. You've got your sloth here to worry about. I get it, you've got rules to follow, and you've got your job. You're a working mother, and I don't blame you for any of this."

That was not what she'd expected him to say. "But I thought—"

"No, forget about what you thought, or what I said to you earlier today. I was a prick. Old feelings came up, and instead of facing the hurt I let myself focus on the anger. I didn't mean any of it. I'm not angry anymore; I see that there are so much more important things going on right now than my bruised ego. If you don't want to tell me what you know about the fires, that's fine. I'll figure out something else, but you're stuck with me, at least for now."

She didn't understand. "You're going to stay?"

He shrugged, looking down at Meg who touched his face and seemed to be exploring the stubble on his cheek and jaw. His smile down at their daughter melted Taylor's heart. "I've got a couple of reasons to stick around now, don't I?"

Not one reason. A couple of reasons. Her heart twisted painfully in her chest.

If this meant there was a real chance...that he didn't hate her for what she'd done...

She shouldn't be that lucky. It seemed impossible that she could be so fortunate after everything that happened between them.

Of course, Taylor probably shouldn't get ahead of herself just yet. There was still the issue to deal with of those fire-starting wolves.

CHAPTER 7

After Jonas finished with Taylor—and even then, he didn't want to leave her—he had to check on the other bear shifters in the community. He grabbed some emergency checklists from his vehicle and headed to the first house.

He was pleased to find many in the community looking to him for guidance and accepting his help. To be fair, there was a good number of them who didn't know him personally, who hadn't been around when he was shunned for being subhuman. Packs and sloths changed more often than the human population liked to think they did. There was some romantic notion of blood brothers, that those within never left, except for matings or death, but that was not always the case.

Nowadays younger members left the nest, so to speak, all the time. Schooling, dating, and shifters who were choosing to live entirely outside the packs were becoming more common than ever. But there were still those who stayed. Those who wanted the prestige that came with being elders in a pack, who wanted to be like those people who had told Taylor to dump him.

Some of the men and women who Jonas recognized seemed a little put out to ask for his advice, to get him into their homes so he could check their fire alarms and emergency packs. He saw more than one clenched fist and tight jaw when he had to explain what else was needed. One home had way too many electrical hazards for his liking, and it hadn't been fun explaining to a bear shifter that he and his mate were putting their cubs in danger by not taking care of that shit.

He was pretty sure he nearly got punched for that, but even if the advice wasn't the sort anyone wanted to hear, the general population put up with it.

Radios were playing in every home, the local news, so everyone would immediately know if there was a call for an evacuation. Those who had an excess of water bottles shared them with those who did not, and when there weren't enough to go around, he had people cleaning and filling empty soda bottles and filling them with tap water.

Even so, he didn't think the people here would evacuate if there were a call for it on the radio or TV. Even if he recommended it. A few might go, those with young children, but in general, shifters were a stubborn sort. He'd need to get Andrew to listen to him, because then if there was a call to evacuate Andrew could make the others go.

But he had to have Andrew on his side.

If he didn't, Jonas already made the choice that he would do anything and everything in his power to get Taylor and their child to come with him.

He wanted to laugh at that. He'd known he was a

father for all of five minutes and already he couldn't stand the thought of leaving Meg here when there were people out there starting these fires.

"You did good, son, really good," Andrew said, clapping him on the back as he was heading back to Taylor's place. It caught Jonas off guard, but he wasn't going to admit to that. He didn't want an alpha knowing he could get the drop on him.

"It might not be enough though. If there's a call to evacuate the area, can I trust that you'll give the order to make them go?"

"What makes you think they wouldn't be going on their own?"

He asked it a little too innocently, and that annoyed Jonas like nothing else.

"Please cut the shit. You and I both know how this works. If there is a call on the radio to evacuate, can I trust that you will command the people here to leave?"

Andrew narrowed his eyes. "I know you like to think we're all a bunch of savage animals, but I can promise you right now, if I think it's too dangerous, I'm sure as hell not going to make anyone stay."

"Uh huh, I'll ask you again because you want to pretend that I'm an idiot and that I'm entirely human." He didn't like that suggestion, and he wanted to make sure Andrew knew it, too. "If there is a call to evacuate, will you give the command for people to leave? I don't care who wants to stay, and I don't care how much you want them to stay; I want to hear you say that you will make them leave."

Andrew looked at him, and something gripped his spine and held on hard. A look like that, from an alpha, it got Jonas somewhere right in his gut. A muffled instinct he suspected had to do with the side of him that belonged to these people. To the shifters in general.

He was being stared at by an alpha. By a male who was stronger than he was and who could snap him in half if he really wanted.

Unlike any other shifters, the beta males and females, or the kids, Jonas was able to fight against the urge to bow his head and submit.

He was only part shifter. Not human enough for the humans to call him a human, and not enough of a shifter to change his form or be taken in by any of the shifters.

It did come with its perks, though, and the ability to resist submitting to the alpha was one of them.

Andrew smirked, crossing his massive arms over his chest, as though trying to remind Jonas of his size. "Sometimes I forget that you were such a stubborn one."

"If you hadn't kicked my mother out of the sloth then it wouldn't have been an issue."

"I never kicked her out. She left after your worthless father did, let's get that straight right now." Andrew's eyes blazed with fire. Jonas nearly fell back a step, and he couldn't believe something so heated, other than an actual fire, was directed at him. "She was ashamed of herself for trusting that no-good loser and didn't want to face anyone in the sloth. Not like she went far anyway; you were always around. You and Taylor got along just fine."

"Until the elders convinced her to dump me when she was pregnant with my kid." He clenched his hands. He wanted to fly at the man, wanted to tear his throat out and demand to know why Andrew had let it all go down like that. As angry as he'd been with Taylor, Jonas could lay a lot of this shit at Andrew's feet, too. "You could have talked her out of it. You could have stopped her, or let me know what was going on."

Andrew sneered at him. "You didn't have a right to know shit. She's the mother. If she didn't want you knowing, you had no business knowing."

"Horseshit."

Andrew shrugged. "Take it up with the courts then. It's not my business anymore anyway." He started to walk off, but Jonas wasn't done. He'd finished checking up on Taylor and Meg and made sure the parents in this damned shithole were packed up if they needed to leave. Now the only task remaining was finding some answers for himself. He saw red and moved in front of Andrew, blocking off the man's path.

He wasn't moving a damned step without them.

"What are you doing?"

"I'm not moving a fucking step until you tell me why you didn't intervene. Jesus Christ, did Taylor tell you what the elders wanted her to do?"

"Yes, she did."

The cold, dead-eyed way Andrew revealed that bit of information had him jerking back. "You...what? You knew?"

"Of course I knew. I'm her alpha. She had her advice, but she wanted a second opinion."

"And she went to you with this?"

"She did."

"And you didn't stop her?"

"It wasn't my decision."

"You're the fucking alpha! Of course it was your decision!"

Sloth members who were outside their house and within earshot stopped what they were doing to look to their alpha, and to the subhuman who was shouting at him. They decided better of it though because they quickly looked away and got right back to packing their items against the checklists Jonas had handed out.

Andrew stared at him with that cold, uncaring look on his face, the one Jonas had gotten used to ever since he was a little kid, sitting on the outskirts of the sloth, wishing he could be within, wondering why his mom wouldn't take him when he was at least half a bear shifter.

He didn't know the rules then. He knew them now, and it pissed him off that those rules had kept him from his child.

Had almost prevented Meg from being here before she was even born.

Andrew took a breath, as though he was the one who was trying to be civil. "It was not my decision what Taylor did with her life or her body. I'm her alpha, not her father or her keeper. If she didn't want to be a mother, if she wanted to get rid of the pregnancy or give Meg up for adoption, I wasn't going to tell her otherwise or judge her for it."

"She was being taken for a ride by the elders. They were giving her shit advice and scaring her into thinking having a subhuman's baby was the worst thing in the world. You could have given her some reassurance."

"I also could have driven her to an abortion clinic and acted as her emotional support there instead of at home. She was an adult and perfectly capable of making her own decisions. I let her do that. I didn't push her one way or the other. I made it clear that this was her life and her decision. That's what an alpha does. I don't control the people here."

Jonas couldn't believe it. "Yes, you do. That's why you didn't ask her to tell me, and that's why you're not going to do shit for these people if there's a call to evacuate."

Andrew chuckled at that, a deceptively friendly noise.

Jonas knew he was trained for heavy lifting, he was fast and stronger than the average human thanks to being a half breed, but even he was shocked by the strength and speed Andrew snapped his hand forward. Just like that, his throat was in a tight iron grip, and Andrew had him yanked forward, their noses practically touching.

"Now you listen to me, and you listen good, you little sack of shit. I did not force her to do anything. Just because I also didn't force her to do what you would have wanted me to do doesn't mean I am in charge of what happened. It's her life. She's in command of it, and you're in command of yours." Andrew shoved Jonas away from him. Jonas stumbled but held his ground. "Maybe if you would have learned not to talk so openly about how terrible all of us are, your girlfriend might not have thought it was a waste to have your kids."

Jonas' throat burned. He clenched his hands, his body tight, ready to go on the attack. Andrew could see it. His smile annoyed Jonas that much more.

"You want to give shifters all kinds of shit for judging you, but you judge us just the same. Do you want to talk about how the elders control the people around here? You want me to control the people here? You just want me to make them do what you want them to do. Where's the difference?"

"You mother—"

"What's going on here?"

Jonas stopped himself before he could say, or do, anything that would have an entire group of bears coming down on him like he owed them money. He turned to see Taylor with Meg in her arms, the baby bag she'd packed over her shoulder.

"Are we leaving?"

Taylor shook her head. "No, not that I'd heard. What were you two doing?" He didn't understand why she would be walking around with the baby bag if she didn't need to have it with her at that moment, but clearly, that wasn't what the issue was here.

"We were just having a friendly chat, nothing to worry about. Right, Jonas?"

Jonas wanted to growl at the man. He still wanted to fight, to get this buildup of rage out of his system, but he didn't. He couldn't. Not with Meg right there.

"Yeah, that's what we were doing." Jonas didn't like Andrew's accusation that Jonas was no better, or that he wanted to control everyone as much as he claimed Andrew already did. Andrew may claim not to control his sloth, but the elders sure as hell had a lot of sway, and he could definitely manipulate the people around him if he wanted to.

Taylor looked at both of them as though she wasn't sure what to believe. Meg's eyes were sliding shut before she forced them back open again and again to stay awake, but it was clear she was going to conk out at any minute.

Jonas looked from them towards the mountain. The smoke was starting to billow a little harder, and more planes were flying in to deal with the fire. If they worked fast enough, had suppressant and a crew already up there to dig a line around the fire, then it could be controlled without spread or other issues.

But it was always better to prepare for the worst. Jonas wanted to be up there with them, and he felt a sense of pride as he watched the hatch of the planes opening up to dump onto the fire. He was hoping the team up there would have their job done quickly, but this wasn't just a campfire put out incorrectly. An accidental fire was one thing, but an intentional one was another. If whoever had done this wanted this to spread...

No. He had to have faith that the team up there would get the job done and stop the fire from heading their way. It was already bad enough that there already was a fire that came a little too close to Lakeview, and this territory in general.

Jonas clenched his teeth. "If either of you has any idea who's causing that," he pointed to the smoke in the distance, "then you both need to tell me what's going on — no more of this bullshit. Taylor, I don't care what Andrew said, what the elders said, or what the people in this sloth want. I care about you, and I care about her." He nodded to Meg. "This could hurt her. This could kill her."

Taylor flinched.

Jonas stepped closer. "The sooner we get a name, the sooner we can put this to bed. My chief is working with the police on this. They can help you even if this is some sort of pack fighting."

"It's not that simple," she said.

"Taylor." There was a warning note in Andrew's voice.

Jonas shook his head, getting in front of Andrew, so Taylor was looking at him instead. "Taylor, if you know anything about what's going on here, and I'm willing to bet you do, then you are actively putting your...our daughter in danger. I know that's not what you want to do here, so please, for the love of God, either tell me or tell the police. If you don't, then I promise that I will do everything in my power to get custody of Meg from you."

Taylor gasped, and the angry, warning growl behind him let Jonas know he'd crossed a line.

Didn't matter. He wasn't going to walk it back. He was serious about this, and he wanted Taylor to know it, too.

"You've got until the end of the day to give me your answer. If you don't give me something to work with, then I'll leave here and get the process started. I can promise you that much."

CHAPTER 8

Jonas moved to his truck. He just completely turned his back to her, as if she was ever going to let him get away with that shit.

"You all right?"

Taylor shook her head. "Andrew, hold Meg."

"Come on, now. You don't want to do anything—"

"I said, you need to hold her." She kept her voice calm, didn't raise it, but Meg groaned a little all the same.

It was a good thing she was tired and getting ready for her nap; otherwise, Taylor didn't want to think of how her daughter would react to the vibes Taylor was giving off right now.

She wanted to murder Jonas.

Andrew took Meg and the baby bag. He was the alpha, in command of this sloth of bears and the safety of the people here. She'd never seen that sort of worry in his eyes, even when she'd had her crisis over whether or not to tell Jonas she was pregnant.

She couldn't focus on that train of thought for long.

She was already marching after Jonas, catching him just as he got the door to his truck open and reached inside.

Taylor's claws were out as she grabbed him by the back of his neck, yanking him out, slamming him against the side of the truck.

His eyes were wide. She swung at him. He dodged out of the way, which infuriated her all the more.

"You bastard! You fucking bastard!"

She swung again, and again, he ducked out of the way.

It wasn't fair. Andrew had been able to take Jonas by the throat so easily, but he was an alpha, a grizzly bear. She was neither an alpha nor a grizzly. She was a black bear. Even if Jonas was a subhuman, the side of him that was a grizzly gave him enough speed to avoid her punches and her claws.

Which was beyond enraging when she wanted nothing more than to slice his face off.

"You're not taking her from me! She's mine! You understand me?"

She punched again but was clumsier about it this time. And angrier. Taylor threw her back into it, and when Jonas ducked his face out of the way, she punched right through the glass of his back window.

And she yowled with pain.

Blinding. White-hot. She sobbed at the blood even as she pulled her hand back to have a look at the damage.

One of her knuckles looked…a little messed up. Oh God. She'd done that, and every second that went by made it all worse and worse.

"Taylor," Jonas reached for her. She yanked herself back.

She didn't want the sympathy in his eyes or the gentle

tone of his voice. Not after he threatened to take Meg from her.

"Don't touch me."

Jonas pulled his hands back. He looked uncomfortable, and it wasn't fair for him to do that. He had no right to look sad or unnerved about anything right now.

"Can we talk inside?"

"No. Go away. Get out of here."

He looked at her pointedly. "You remember what I said I would do if I left here without the answers I wanted, right?"

Taylor clenched her teeth.

She looked back at Andrew. He still held Meg protectively. A few people watched what had taken place with fixed attention, but there were others who were trying not to pay attention. They weren't doing such a great job of minding their own damned business, though. She could tell what they were doing. They were doing such a terrible job of pretending not to watch what was going on that it was insane.

"Taylor, come on. We can talk inside. Please."

She hated him so much right now. "What was all that back at my place? You said you were sorry. You made it out as if you forgave me for..."

Even angry with him, she didn't want to say it, and she flinched at the reminder that she wasn't entirely innocent in this either.

"I do forgive you. I..." He sighed. "Taylor, please, I know you love that little girl. I want to get to know her." He leaned in close, lowering his voice. "If anything happens to her because you didn't let me help, that option won't be on the table anymore. I can protect you. I can protect Meg. I can."

The worst part was she knew he was right. Even if there was a backlash to bringing the humans into this, it didn't change the fact that there was a fire being put out within sight of her home.

She didn't want to worry about Meg's safety. From the wolves, or the fire. The thing was, she could hide from wolves, but even the smallest of children were taught there was no hiding from a fire.

"Andrew?"

"Yeah?"

She looked back at her alpha. He had to know what she was thinking, what she was planning on doing. It had to be written all over her face.

And she'd left her daughter in his arms.

"I'm going to put Meg to bed now."

He looked at her, the wheels turning in his head.

Taylor found herself holding her breath without meaning to.

When he stepped forward, putting Meg into her arms, her little body slumping against her chest in sleep, Taylor felt stupid for thinking the worst of her alpha.

Andrew handed Meg's bag to Jonas. "You do what you've got to do. I'll work something out later."

He meant with the sloth — the people who weren't going to be happy with her decision.

And there would be enough of them to make things difficult for her later on.

Taylor wanted to cry. She really did.

She lowered her head instead, making sure no one could see her eyes. At least not yet.

"Jonas, let's talk inside."

Jonas glanced up towards the fire, the planes still rumbling as they went to and from the fire itself. She didn't see flames, only smoke, and steam. She hoped that meant it was being controlled before it could grow like the last fire.

Still, she wasn't a bad mom. Her little girl against her chest hit it home for her. How much she wanted to give Meg everything. How she couldn't handle the idea of even sort of putting her into harm's way.

That wasn't what she wanted to do, and that wasn't who she was. Not in the least.

She went inside. Jonas followed her, and so did the eyes of everyone in her sloth, all of them knowing she was about to get the humans involved.

* * *

"You should let me see your hand."

"It's fine."

"You're bleeding." Jonas didn't like that. He didn't have the same heightened senses. Not all of them, anyway, but the blood looked a little redder than he would have liked.

The fact that she got that when her eyes had been that same shade of red, when her face had been sprouting fur and fangs popping out from her teeth, because of him, made it even worse.

"Let me have a look. If it's broken, you don't want it healing wrong."

Taylor dragged a baby play mat over to them and put Meg down onto it. The little girl settled onto her back, eyes closed, completely asleep.

Jonas stepped up beside Taylor and reached for her hand, taking it in his. She pressed her lips together, but she allowed him to touch her anyway.

"This will hurt, but just bear with me."

Her mouth quirked.

He didn't comment on the accidental pun. He focused on prodding her knuckle, making sure it didn't feel out of place.

She hissed; a little blood got on his fingers. "Not broken. Come on; we can wash it in the sink."

"It hurts a lot."

"We'll make sure there's no glass in there. Come on."

She didn't fight him. He was grateful for that.

With her hand beneath the tap, he couldn't help but smile. "I can't believe you smashed my window."

Taylor ducked her head. "I'm sorry about that. I'll pay for it."

He wasn't sure if she would have the money for that, but he didn't mention it.

Luckily, there was no glass. All she needed was a towel over the small wound, and she was good to go.

"I'm sorry for saying I'd take her, but you know I'd only do it to keep her safe, right?"

Taylor nodded.

"And that's not a dig against you as a mother either. If I were doing anything that could hurt that little girl, I'd expect you to do the same with me or anyone else she was in contact with."

"I know."

She just didn't sound happy about it.

He didn't blame her for it.

"I mean it. If the sloth can't take having humans

involved, I'll take you with me. We'll leave here together—you, me, and Meg. I've got a nice place. It's comfortable there."

"But it's not territory."

This was one of the few things he never understood about full-blooded shifters. The need some have to be surrounded by their own when others could handle living outside of their packs just fine. What were they doing differently?

"You're right, though." Taylor looked up at Jonas. "I'm...I'm going to get her hurt if I can't separate myself from all of this. She's a baby. She can't protect herself, and the last fire was so close."

"We won't let anything happen to her."

"But what if something happens to the people here because I said something? There are other kids here, Jonas. Other babies. If I get them hurt or killed because I wanted to protect Meg, doesn't that make me a bad mother? Even if they're not my kids?"

"I don't think so. You would be protecting your own. That's a natural thing to do. But you care. You're not heartless. You just have to make a decision. Your child, or someone else's. If the parents here can't be bothered to take their kids away from the dangers coming, that is not on you."

She flinched. Jonas clenched her shoulders, leaning down just enough to look her in the eye, to put them on the same level.

"But I'll do everything I can to make sure that doesn't happen either. We'll do everything possible to keep the people here safe, even if someone tries to retaliate. Okay?"

Taylor exhaled a long breath, relief clouding her eyes.

"There was fighting, between a pack of wolves, not too long ago."

Finally. This was it. This was the information his chief needed, that the police needed.

"Tell me whatever you can. When you're done, we can take Meg and get out of here, just you and me. We'll make sure all of this comes to a stop."

Taylor shook her head, bringing back that sense of unease within him. "It's not that easy. Things have been different since you left."

"I know. I know there was a murder investigation not too long ago."

That would have an impact on the local communities. Even groups of shifters could become victim to the fears that came with hearing their towns and communities weren't so safe anymore.

Taylor nodded. "Did you hear what else happened?"

That didn't sound good. "I heard there were arrests made. And that someone was illegally turned into a shifter." Some states required a license to turn a human into a shifter. Others introduced prison time if it was done against the will of the former human involved. But he didn't get the feeling that was the bit Taylor was worried about.

"Later on, the man who was changed, I guess he found a conduit. Do you know what that is?"

Jonas bit back on a growl. "Yeah, I know what a conduit is."

He'd never seen one in person. He wasn't even sure what the exact rules were when it came to them.

Supposedly, they were in a category similar to subhumans. Only they weren't born conduits. They were humans who had been attacked by a wolf, or bear, or any shifter. But unlike most, who would become shifters after an attack, their transformation didn't take.

Not only that it didn't take, but it changed their scent, making them more desirable to other shifters.

Jonas heard a rumor that anyone who mated with a conduit received a massive boost in strength. Their hearing and sight improved dramatically. Others said the children born from a union were the ones who benefited with power.

The story was rarely straight when it came to them. They weren't exactly as common as subhumans.

"So what happened with the conduit?"

"I guess the wolves that changed the male she was with didn't like that she was with anyone. Look, I don't know the exact details, but a group of wolves came here not so long ago. It was just meant to be a visit with Andrew, to talk about resources, what we could buy and sell. No one had a good feeling about them."

Calm. Jonas felt oddly calm hearing this. Not because it wasn't important, but because he was starting to get to a place where he could do something about it all. There was something about this that made a monster within his chest rumble and gave him a deep, simmering desire to find whoever these bastards were and bring them to justice. Just the idea that these men had been anywhere near Taylor...near his daughter... it was enough to make something dangerous ignite within him.

"Did you see what they looked like?"

"From a distance. I got their scent though."

He cringed. "That's not so much help for me, but maybe we could do something with it. There's always a couple of cops who are shifters." He glanced to Meg, making sure she was still sleeping before giving his full attention back to Taylor. "What did they want? Are you sure they're the ones who started the fire?"

Taylor nodded, pressing her lips together as she glanced down. "Yeah. I didn't know at first, but...Andrew told me. After."

He fucking knew it.

"Don't be mad."

"How can I not be angry?"

The only reason why he wasn't stomping around, cursing up a storm, or grabbing Taylor and kissing her hard on the mouth, was because his child was sleeping mere feet away from him.

"What did they say? Did Andrew tell you what they wanted?"

She nodded. "Yeah. They want our help finding their conduit, and taking over a skulk of foxes. Andrew declined, then the fires started. They're a warning, Jonas. The burned trees on the way up here? Those happened when someone did try to leave. The wolves brought them back, Jonas. We're trapped here, and we can't get the humans involved."

CHAPTER 9

Jonas had a walk around the area where the first fires occurred. He checked the underbrush that remained—dry and singed in some places, dead trees that should have been cut down a long time ago to prevent this sort of thing.

Had it not been for the rain, this could have been much worse.

"What are you looking for?"

Jonas glanced behind him. Taylor stood right there, jeans, a t-shirt, and hiking boots—never looked better. Her hair was tied back, the blue streaks glinting in the sunlight. "What are you doing here? Where's Meg?"

Taylor stepped over some dried roots and branches, her boots crunching on the ones she couldn't avoid. "She's safe. With Andrew. I don't think you're going to find out how the fires started."

"I'm not looking for that. I don't think it matters much right now anyway."

"Really?" Taylor came up to stand beside him. She

knelt, surveying the scene with intense eyes. As if she thought there could be some clue hidden within the damage, even though she told him he'd find nothing.

"I'm checking to see how bad it might be if another fire came through here."

"It sounds like they've got the one up the hill mostly contained."

Which was no reason to relax. He wished she would stay with Meg, but Jonas knew better than to tell her that. Taylor had a stubborn streak. She could dig her heels in when she wanted to, and he wasn't about to risk that when the situation was as…delicate as it was.

"So, how bad could another fire get? I mean, it doesn't look like it's going to rain for a little while again, but the local fire department seems to be on it."

Jonas nodded. "Yeah, I might need to make a trip up there later."

From his peripheral vision, Jonas saw the way she jerked back.

"Up there? You mean, up there, up there? For real?"

As she said it, the rumble of a helicopter engine burred overhead, carrying another load of suppressant with it towards the billowing smoke.

Jonas stood, smacking his hands together to dislodge the dirt and soot. "Yeah."

She stood with him. "Wait, are you serious? Isn't that dangerous?"

He headed for his truck. "More fire departments rely on volunteers. If they need the extra manpower around here because of your wolf friends, then I want to know about it."

Taylor chased after him. "My wolf friends? Okay,

going to ignore that for now, but I will talk with you about that later."

Fuck. He shouldn't have opened his mouth.

"But aren't you trained to put out house fires? Apartments that catch, car crashes, cats in trees, that sort of thing? Isn't this entirely different?"

"I could still be of use."

He got into the driver's side of his truck, shut the door, started the ignition, and slid the window down. He looked at Taylor. She looked worried. It was in her eyes. In the way her feet seemed to fidget and the way she didn't seem to know what to do with her hands.

"I'm not leaving you, if that's what you're thinking."

"That is absolutely not what I'm thinking."

Was that the truth? He couldn't tell. She'd gotten good at hiding things from him.

"I'm not leaving Meg either, if that's what you're worried about."

She shook her head. "No, I know you wouldn't do that. Now that you know." She smiled at him, a weak, watery smile.

He could barely return it. He didn't want to deal with the heavy load of what it meant that he'd missed out on the first year and a half of his daughter's life any more than Taylor did.

"I'm so sorry about that. I really thought it was for the best at the time and—"

"We're good. Trust me, it's fine."

Taylor snapped her lips shut. She seemed to shrink in a little.

Jonas sighed. "Did you come here in your bear form?"

Taylor nodded. "I heard you'd left. Not that I was

trying to catch you or anything. I just wanted to see if you needed anything. Help, I mean, with…" She gestured around her. "Everything that's been going on. You know?"

Jonas nodded, watching her. Had she been worried he wasn't coming back? He didn't want to admit that made him feel pretty good.

"Yeah, I know. You want to come with me?"

Her expression changed. Seemed to get more…open. "Yeah? Really? Wait, won't I get in the way?"

"Not if you're willing to tell the chief of police what you just told me."

She closed up again, backing up a step. "Jonas…I don't think I can do that."

"I've got to tell the people in charge everything you told me. Having your first-hand account will make things easier." He waited a beat. "Taylor, I won't let anything happen to Meg. Not a thing."

He surprised himself with the intensity of how he said it. Jonas had known he was a father for all of five minutes, and yet everything inside of him screamed at him that he needed to protect that little girl from now until the day he died. He wasn't ready yet to examine the strength of his need to protect and care for Taylor too, but it was up there.

And he wasn't about to let some fire-happy wolf shifters playing with lighters hurt his family.

He reached over, pushing open the passenger side door. "Taylor, come on. We have to end this. This can't go on."

Another burr of a helicopter sounded above them. Taylor looked towards it, then him before walking around the front of the truck and climbing into the passenger seat.

"If I'm going to do this, then you should hurry and get me to whoever it is you want me to talk to. Before I think better of it and change my mind."

Jonas grinned and put the truck in gear. "Yes, ma'am."

Jonas' tires got off the gravel and onto the road when Taylor spoke again, her voice much quieter than what he was used to.

"After, if you wanted, I think we should talk a little. About everything that happened."

Jonas clenched his jaw. He couldn't exactly help it. "Yeah. I think you're right."

Taylor sighed, putting her elbow up onto the window of the truck, resting her chin on her fist. "Then, after that, we should find somewhere private to have sex."

He thought about that for about a half second, his pulse immediately picking up as the hairs on his arms and back of his neck stood on end.

"Yeah, I think that sounds like a plan."

CHAPTER 10

Taylor stayed quiet in the truck, observing that Jonas seemed to know his way around. Her area of the world was small, and he'd had time to get aquatinted with everything before he'd met up with her at the daycare, so she supposed it made sense.

She couldn't stop her heart from pounding, and Taylor had to repeatedly remind herself that Meg was safe and sound with Andrew. He wouldn't let anything happen to her while she was away. That didn't keep her anxiety at bay though, and a part of her wished she'd taken her daughter with her. Andrew might be strong, but a protective mama bear would stop at nothing to protect their cub.

"Are we going to the police right now?"

"Yes and no. We're heading to your fire station. My chief will be there. I sent him a text saying I was coming. He doesn't know you're with me yet."

She nodded. It made sense. She hadn't seen him pull

out his phone since she showed up. "The old fire station was upgraded, you know, it's not where you think it is."

"I know. I had a look around before I came to find you."

Taylor nodded. "Right."

This was a little too awkward. She'd thought she would be lightening the mood when she told Jonas she wanted to have sex with him, but that lasted for all of two minutes before they went back to this tricky spot they were in now.

"So, how dangerous are these wolves exactly? Do you have names?"

Taylor looked at Jonas, then away as she wet her lips. "I have a few names."

Jonas briefly glanced away from the road, looking right at her before he started paying attention again. "You know I won't let anything happen to Meg, right?"

Taylor nodded. "I know you'll do everything possible to keep something from happening to her, but—"

"But nothing. I won't let anything happen to her."

"You're not in control of everything, Jonas. Things happen that are outside of our limits all the time. This might be one of those times, and I'm just thinking about… the future."

A future where she might have to get her daughter and flee this damned town and everyone in it pronto.

Jonas nodded. "Right. I got it."

"I'm not saying you wouldn't be part of that future if you wanted to be around."

"Okay, since we're on that subject, yes. I do want to be around, and don't want to miss out on any more time with my daughter."

Taylor cringed.

What little they'd already spoken about Meg, and their separation, wouldn't be enough. Taylor knew she had so much more to answer for. She'd been so sure Jonas wouldn't want anything to do with a shifter child that she'd just watched him walk away. So sure he wanted his own life away from her and the sloth. Now she was here, sitting next to the man she'd loved, coming to grips with the fact that she did still love him.

She still wanted him. Raising her daughter and being part of the sloth, working for her living, and then having to deal with the wolves, all of it had given her enough to think about that she managed to pack away her feelings for Jonas. She'd had woken up, cared for her daughter, went to work, then sleep, then started all over again for so many days that she'd managed to convince herself she was satisfied with her life, and over Jonas MacBride.

No. Having him here, and telling him about Meg, and taking in his scent while he sat next to her, brought everything back to the forefront of her mind. She couldn't ignore this.

Which meant making things right, starting with the wolves causing the fires, and then dealing with Jonas.

Though Lakeview was a small town, Taylor almost never stopped by the fire station. She used to drive by the old one when she foolishly hoped that Jonas would turn up working there someday. She'd indulge herself in these moments, thinking about him, and then parking and looking at their old text conversations. She wasn't about to tell him this though; she didn't want to sound weird or anything.

The new fire station was quiet. It made sense, as most,

if not all of the people working there would be focused on the fire already burning, or cutting down the underbrush nearby to keep it from spreading.

"Is there anyone even here?" she asked, even though the garage doors were wide open.

"There are some here. My chief would have met up with them to see if there was anything our department could do to help. Come on."

Taylor pressed her lips together and got out of the truck. She scratched at her arm, looking down, and seeing some of her fur poking through her pores. To calm herself and regain control she inhaled a deep breath, exhaled, and then breathed deeply again. This wasn't going to be so bad. It was ultimately for Meg's safety and the safety of the people who lived in and around Lakeview.

She could do this.

She hoped.

Taylor had never seen the inside of this fire station before. It didn't look like anything she'd seen on TV. It was just a long brick building, new, but still with the expected tells of a fire station.

Jonas walked right into the garage, and she followed. The building was new, but the fire truck looked as though it needed replacing. It was probably as old as it was allowed to be before a replacement was mandatory. She could make out many smells from the people who had been here. While some shifters could be overwhelmed by the scents of too many people all at once, Taylor handled it better than others. She'd developed a tolerance for it after working with so many children at her daycare, but this was different.

She had a no-scent policy at the daycare, which not

only helped her but also helped the sensitive noses of her little charges. There was no such policy at the police station though. She could smell the pheromones of many men, a few women, shifter and human alike, intermingled with each other as well as with different kinds of after-shave and perfumed deodorants. On top of that, the garage held the strong scent of motor oil, grease, and tire rubber from trucks.

Even so, another scent came at her through the thick soup of smells. Something metallic and familiar.

What is that?

Jonas stopped short right in the doorway leading to another part of the station. "Fuck me."

He bolted forward.

"What? Hey! Jonas where are you—" Taylor stopped short when she came to the doorway.

It looked like the lounge. There was a television going. The fire was on the news with video of the helicopters flying overhead, dumping water and suppressant onto the flames while other men and women dug long ditches around the fire, preventing the spread.

That wasn't what she was paying attention to. On the floor, she realized what the smell was that she'd come across.

Blood. A decent amount of it, too. Jonas flew into action, knowing instantly what he needed to do. Taylor stayed back, knowing better than to contaminate a crime scene.

"Fuck, Dallas? Chief, come on."

Taylor blinked. Somewhere in the distance, Jonas yelled for her, but she couldn't look away. She didn't see the people on the floor anymore. Not as they were. She saw Andrew. She saw the elders of her sloth, her customers, her child. Meg was sitting right there, her little white diaper and chubby legs stained with blood. Her little fist, covered in blood, was to her mouth as she sucked on her hand, all the while looking up at Taylor with those wide, innocent eyes…

Jonas pulled out his phone and dialed while Taylor stood where she was, utterly useless as the sound of everything around her slipped farther and farther away.

"Taylor!"

Taylor snapped out of it, but only when Jonas gripped her by the shoulders and started to push her out of the room.

"You with me?"

She blinked up at him, then shook her head. "Yeah. Yeah, I'm sorry. I…what can I do?"

Jonas glanced back into the room, then at her. "I'd ask you to help me administer first aid, but if you're going to go into shock, it's not going to help anyone. Why don't you step out front and wait out front for an ambulance to get here? You can bring them to me."

She didn't think the paramedics would have trouble finding this place. They weren't out in the woods, so it wouldn't take long, and they would be familiar with the area. He was trying to get rid of her, and after her near panic attack, she couldn't blame him.

"All right." She glanced over his shoulder into the room, tried to, but Jonas took her chin, his grip gentle yet firm as he forced her attention back onto him. "You don't have to look at that."

"Are they dead?"

"I might be able to help some, but the quicker the ambulance gets here, the better. Go on now."

Any other time, Taylor wouldn't have left. She liked to think of herself as being the strong, independent type. She was trained in first aid. She knew how to dislodge food stuck in a toddler's throat, and she had tried herself to be a little obsessive compulsive when it came to keeping anything with peanuts out of her building.

But this was different, and there was nothing that could be solved by sticking around if she was going to freeze up and take Jonas' attention away from the victims. She glanced back towards the lounge. She could hear Jonas inside, speaking to someone. That meant one of them had to be alive. She hoped at least one of them was still alive.

If Taylor couldn't do something for the people in there, then she could do something for them out here. She put her nose to the air and started to get a better whiff, searching through the oil, the chemicals, and the aftershaves.

If this had anything to do with Maxwell's pack, she was going to figure out what it was. She already had a good idea, but if any of the scents here matched the scents she already knew…

"What are you doing?"

Taylor snapped her attention up at the figure entering the garage. A woman with the pointed fox ears and tail, looking right at her.

CHAPTER 11

She was beautiful. Even with the turtleneck on, the tight jeans and hiking boots, it was clear this was a knockout. Taylor wasn't sure why this was the first thing she noticed about the other woman, but it annoyed her, and the fact that this chick was here when there were people hurt in the back…

Wait.

The fox girl took a step forward.

Taylor straightened her back and made sure this chick could see her claws, too.

"Don't take another step."

Fox girl stopped, her eyes flying wide, and then she stepped back. "Okay, uh, I'm not here to start trouble."

Yeah, right.

"What are you doing here? Did you have anything to do with what happened to these men?"

The fox frowned. "Happened to who?" Her eyes flew wide. "Where is Victor?"

Taylor shook her head, not willing to let this woman trick her. "Don't know who that is, but you're not going to take another step until the police get here."

Even now she could hear sirens coming, which eased some of her tension. The fox girl took the slight distraction and marched forward.

Taylor stepped towards her. "You're not going back there."

Jonas was trying to save lives. This bitch might've had something to do with the bloodshed, and she wasn't about to let her get anywhere near her man.

The fox was shorter than Taylor, and the turtleneck didn't give off the impression of bravery, so Taylor was stunned when the woman's eyes started to glow, and her long fox ears twitched. "You're going to want to get the fuck out of my way."

Taylor pressed her lips together. "You're talking to a bear here. You don't want to be throwing your weight around, fox."

There weren't many times when it was better to be a bear, but Taylor loved it right then. Wolves, foxes, and even the cats, always had a sleeker, sexier nature about them. They had ears and tails that were sharper and longer. Taylor always envied the cute fluff to a fox tail over her own little bear ball. But, this time around, the added strength that came with being a bear was something she would embrace to the fullest for the safety of Jonas and the victims he was helping.

The fox girl pressed her lips together, her eyes darting towards the door.

"Don't even think about it."

The fox woman vibrated a rage that Taylor had rarely seen in anyone else. Her hands clenched to fists, her tail whipping around behind her.

"My mate might be back there. I want to make sure he's all right. I can smell blood. Please let me through."

There was never a more unhappy 'please' said in the entire world. That meant something, considering Taylor worked with babies and toddlers who needed to be coaxed to say it on many occasions.

But it was the M word the fox said that made Taylor rethink her position. She could be lying, trying to trick Taylor, but having another woman standing there, asking to be let through because her mate might be in trouble…

If she were in that situation, Taylor would forge her way through anyone who tried to stop her from getting to Jonas.

With a whole lot of blood.

Taylor pressed her lips together. "There are some people back there in pretty bad shape."

Which was the wrong thing to say because the fox girl tried pushing through her. "Then let me see him!"

"Hold on, hold on, your mate might not be back there. He could be fine. I don't know you, and you could mess up the…scene."

That's what the police said about these sorts of things, right? They didn't want someone showing up and stomping all over a crime scene, right?

Shit. The sirens were coming closer. Taylor glanced towards the open garage doors, which was a mistake because the fox girl pushed passed Taylor before she could grab onto her.

"Shit."

"Victor? Victor!"

"Wait!"

The woman ran into the lounge, following her nose. She was way too fast for Taylor to catch up to before she ran into the room.

Taylor stopped in the doorway and saw Jonas sit up to look to the fox woman and then to Taylor. "Where did she come from?"

The fox woman stopped in front of one of the men. He wore a grey suit, he could have been a police officer, but he wasn't dressed the way the other men were. Not in any noticeable uniform.

"Victor? Baby? Shit, come on."

"Don't move him. Don't move him!"

It was too late. The fox woman turned the man over onto his back. A groan came from him, which was lucky; he was all right. Hopefully, nothing else would happen after being moved like that.

Mated pairs tended to feed off of each other. Energies were shared, which allowed humans who mated with shifters to have slightly faster healing times. Still, the fox woman's touch on his cheek shouldn't have been enough to make the injured man open his eyes. But it was.

She smiled down at him, her eyes brimming with tears. The man, Victor, looked back at her as though he was drunk and high at the same time. "What are you doing here?" Victor slurred his words.

The fox woman laughed. "You weren't answering your texts. I was worried."

Taylor and Jonas looked at each other, and Taylor's gut

clenched. That was how a mate behaved. That was the worry and love of a mate.

A mate didn't turn her back on the one she loved.

Taylor pushed the thought away. For the moment. She had to. There was too much else to think about, now that she knew this woman was not about to go on a killing spree. There was no time to discuss anything though, because the next thing Taylor knew, there were shouts. She was commanded to put her hands in the air, which she did right away.

The fox girl refused to take her hands away from her mate, and Jonas, his voice as commanding and strong as ever, called out to the men in blue to let them know who he was and what he was doing.

They were all instructed to move away from the victims while paramedics came to tend to the dead and dying. Taylor couldn't help but think it was for the best. These people didn't just have the training, but they also had better equipment on hand. And she was just happy to be taken away from all the blood.

* * *

JONAS GRIT his teeth as he was asked for the fifth time his full name, where he lived, and what he did for his living. He knew this tactic had to work from time to time; otherwise, the detectives questioning him wouldn't ever use it. They were only covering their bases and making sure they had all the details.

Still, he couldn't stand this. Being hauled off to the station for questioning was one thing, but being separated from Taylor was even worse. He knew the scene shook her, and he wanted to be able to comfort her and reassure her that everything was going to be okay. Something he couldn't do before, at the scene while there were so many people he needed to try to help.

Detective Grey looked young, almost too young to be a detective, which meant he was either older than he looked or he'd risen through the ranks incredibly fast. Regardless, the man looked at Jonas as if he was the prime suspect in his case now, which Jonas almost couldn't blame him for.

"You're telling me that you're a lieutenant firefighter with the Astraea Fire Department, and your chief asked you to come down here and question your ex-girlfriend about the fires being set in the area?"

"Yes. That's what I'm here for."

Detective Grey raised a brow, and he turned his attention to the other detective in the room as though to ask if Jonas was serious or not.

"I know it's out of the ordinary, but he brought me along because he knew I had connections to the bear clan in the area."

"You don't look like a shifter to me," Grey said, his gaze darting to the top of Jonas' head, noting the lack of ears.

"Subhuman. I don't shift. I used to live around here. I know this sloth."

"Were you one of theirs?"

Jonas shook his head. "Not officially, no. I was allowed to stick around because my mother was a shifter."

"All right, say we believe you. Did you find anything out about the fires?"

Jonas knew this wouldn't make Taylor feel too good, to have everything Jonas had learned about the situation spilled when she wasn't there to confirm or deny it, but she would forgive him for it.

He hoped.

This was for their daughter.

"It's a wolf pack. Something is going on around here, and you can ask Taylor about it if you want more details. I guess a fight broke out with a fox skulk and a wolf pack after an alpha was killed, then there was a fight for a conduit. The wolf pack wanted the bear clan to back them up, and when they refused the started causing trouble. The fires started after some bears tried to leave the area to get away from all of it."

And from the look in Detective Grey's eyes, Jonas knew he'd said something that the man either already knew, or heavily suspected. "Am I right?"

Grey smiled at him, taking a seat across from him. "We'll look into that. Any idea who the fox woman was? Or the man she was with?"

Jonas shook his head. "I barely got a look at her before she ran in. I was too busy trying to make sure my chief was alive." He glared at the other man, "any updates on his status?"

"When I hear anything back, I'll let you know. The fox woman corroborates your story. She said she never met you or the bear shifter before."

Jonas frowned. "Do you know her?"

Ignoring Jonas' question, Grey leaned back, looked to the other detective in the room with them, and when he reached his hand back, an orange envelope was placed in it. He opened the envelope and carefully spilled the contents onto the table, spreading out pictures and papers.

"Tell me what you know about these wolves."

Taylor had never been questioned by the police before. She didn't like it, and she didn't want to make a habit of it in the future either. There was something about not being in control of when she was able to leave this place that didn't sit well with her on so many levels, especially as they asked her questions she wasn't sure she could answer.

Taylor always thought she could handle situations like this with a certain level of grace. All she had to do was tell the truth as she knew it, but sitting at that table with two officers questioning her...it was a lot different compared to what she thought it would be.

Especially since she knew so much.

Taylor ended up telling them everything she knew about the wolves and the skulk of foxes five times. The worst part was all the questions the detectives kept asking, hoping she'd have more information. She had a general idea of what was going on, but her timelines were somewhat off because she wasn't directly involved. At one point, after what seemed like a thousand years had passed, another detective came into the room, and Taylor barely stopped herself from jumping out of her seat.

"It's been hours. Can I go yet?"

"Soon." The detective nodded to the others, and they left the room, leaving her alone with the new one alone.

"I've got a kid at home, and things are crazy right now. Please, I'm trying to tell you everything I know. I just need to get home."

"My name is Detective Grey. I've already contacted your alpha. He knows where you are, and he's taking good care of, Meg, was it?"

Taylor grit her teeth at the mention of her daughter's name. She didn't know how to take something like that. It didn't sound threatening, not really, but this guy knowing Meg's name while she was stuck here didn't jive well with her.

"Yes, that is her name."

Detective Grey smiled at her, but Taylor still wasn't feeling so impressed. "You don't have to be so alarmed. So far, everything you've said checks out with what your friend said."

"Jonas?" Taylor felt a twinge of pain in her stomach. Of course they questioned Jonas, and he would have told them everything he could about what Taylor already knew. He would have had to. He wasn't part of the sloth anymore, and he lived in a completely different world from her. And he'd already said that he was planning on giving as much information to the police as possible. "If Jonas spoke to you then you know it's not exactly safe for me to be without my baby right now. When can I go home?"

"Soon enough. We're just confirming a few things with the vixen shifter who came into the fire station."

"Right, you can ask her. I wasn't there beforehand, and neither was Jonas; we have no idea what happened to all those people." Jonas had seemed especially concerned about one of them. "Are they all right? He was going to meet with one of his friends."

Detective Grey looked her right in the eyes. "Four people were brought into the hospital alive. One died while being airlifted out; one is currently in stable condition, and the other two are still fighting."

Taylor cringed. She thought of Jonas, thought of the name of his boss. What was it again?

"Was there a man named Dallas? Was he all right? Or at least alive?"

The detective's smile was a kind one, and Taylor couldn't figure out if he was trying to be nice but was unable to say one way or the other, or if he didn't want to give her the bad news. Her stomach clenched. "Anyway, I don't want you or Jonas going far. We're going to need to keep in touch. Some of our wolves are sniffing around the station to see if they can come up with anything."

"Wolves? You had wolves sniffing around the station?"

Grey raised a brow at her. "There a problem with that?"

Taylor couldn't believe he didn't see it. "Well, yeah, kind of. You know it was wolves who did this, that a wolf pack is setting these fires."

Detective Grey stared at her as though he couldn't be less impressed. "You know, it is possible for wolf shifters to come from differing packs. I can promise you that the people who work for us are professionals and they will do their jobs efficiently."

Taylor swallowed a little harder than she was used to, embarrassed. "Right. Yeah, sorry." Shifters had enough trouble with humans continually worrying about being attacked, without her adding to it.

"Come on. I'll take you to the front desk."

Taylor said nothing, standing when the detective prompted her to, following him out of that cold, depressing room while she ruminated on her assumptions about the wolves.

She'd given Jonas so much hell for not wanting to be part of a sloth of bears who were constantly pushing him away. She'd allowed herself to be persuaded by the sloth to give him up when he was one of the best things in her life. Then she'd held against him his frustration with how some packs and sloths behaved towards subhumans. Meanwhile, it took her less than a second before she did the same thing to a group of wolf shifters she'd never even met.

Taylor wanted to get out of here. She wanted to go home to her daughter, and she needed to throw her arms around Jonas' neck and kiss him until she purged herself of this terrible guilt.

She let the detective bring her to the front. She signed her name and then waited for Jonas.

When he came out next, she could hardly look at him. He seemed a little too cool, too calm. She knew he was thinking about Dallas.

"You ready to go?"

She jumped a little. Taylor barely noticed when he'd

walked up to her, but Jonas always had been good at keeping his footsteps light.

She nodded. "Yeah, I want to go."

When they made it outside, Taylor's eyes scanned the hills in the distance. Smoke still plumed, and the helicopters were still flying to and from the area.

"I think they've got it contained. We should be fine."

She blinked at that, following him to his truck. "How can you tell?"

"A couple of reasons. Because we weren't told to evacuate, the recent rains are probably making it hard for the fire to spread too far even with all the underbrush, and these guys are moving fast. Whoever set the fires put the people around here on edge. They were prepared."

Taylor nodded, moving to the passenger side of his truck, which they'd been allowed to take to the station before their questioning.

"Sorry," she said once she'd buckled her seatbelt.

"For what?" Jonas turned the engine.

Taylor wet her lips, trying and failing to not look at the ink on his fingers. "For everything. I should've...I should've gone to the police sooner. I could've done something."

"You think I blame you for what happened to Dallas?"

"He's your friend, isn't he? I mean, not just your boss? Aren't you angry?"

"I am. I'm fucking pissed, and so will the rest of the guys be when they find out, but I'm mad at the wolves that did this, not at you. You're the one being terrorized; you're the one who fell into this. You didn't do anything wrong."

"Oh." That made her feel a little better, but she still

didn't know what to do about…everything else. "Okay then."

Jonas kept right on smiling. "Dallas will be all right. He's a tough old bastard. A subhuman, too, actually. He's not about to let a pack of wolves get the better of him."

Taylor sighed. "That's good."

"The others weren't so lucky."

She cringed. That was right. People had still died, so it wasn't good at all.

"Try not to think about it so much."

"How can I not think about it? This is all my fault."

"How is this even remotely your fault? Let alone all of it?"

Taylor pressed her lips together. "I just…after seeing those people on the floor…don't you at least somewhat blame me? I could have done something so much sooner."

"So could everyone in your sloth. You told me why everyone was keeping quiet about it. I'm telling you, Taylor, I promise you, I don't blame you for this, and you shouldn't blame yourself either. This isn't on you."

Despite his words, she couldn't help but think that it was. At least in some way. It had to be. She'd wanted to protect her home and her daughter, and maybe that would be enough to help her sleep at night, but for now, she wanted to forget.

"Are you going to take me home?"

Jonas nodded. "I think that's the best place for you to be. The police will show up soon after. They might already be there asking questions. I hope you're okay with that."

Taylor nodded. Anyone who had a problem with the humans getting involved at this point could kiss her ass.

She'd seen what the wolves were willing to do, to her people as well as the humans, and she wasn't ready to take the risk. Not anymore.

"Do you think Meg and I could stay with you in the city? At least until all of this blows over."

The corner of Jonas' mouth quirked. "Absolutely."

<h1 style="text-align:center">CHAPTER 13</h1>

*J*onas could tell something was different on the ride back to the sloth. Taylor wasn't usually this withdrawn. She was usually more open. Even her anger would be better than this.

He didn't like to think that the sight of all that blood had traumatized her, or that sitting in a cement room with a two-way mirror for hours on end had finished the job, but there was always that possibility.

He didn't want this for her. He didn't want to come back to upend everything she'd worked for and everything she knew, but even if there were some magical option to turn back time and ease her into this, he wouldn't do it.

He had that little girl to think about.

How strange that he'd only known about Meg for a grand total of fewer than twenty-four hours and he already wanted to protect her with his life. It was as though some powerful instinct had awakened within him, and there was no going back.

That wasn't the only instinct of his that had awakened. Jonas did his damned best to not glance at Taylor as he drove, but it was difficult.

He was a subhuman. He couldn't shift. He didn't have the ears, the tail, or the senses that came with being a shifter, but right at that moment, Jonas was starting to feel more alive than he'd ever felt since leaving this little town.

He shouldn't, but he couldn't help it either. This was a mating pull, and there was no resisting something like that for long.

Not even seeing a good friend struggling for his life.

It stunned him when Taylor was the first to speak up. "You think you could pull over real quick before getting back to the territory?"

Jonas looked at her, gauging the color under her jawline. "You feeling sick?"

Taylor shook her head, her fingernails digging into her thighs. "No, I just want to touch you."

Jonas' heartbeat sped up. By a lot. "You don't have to do anything you don't want to do."

The low growl in Taylor's voice was warning enough. "Please don't patronize me right now. This has nothing to do with what happened back...there. I just don't want to wait anymore. I need to feel you."

They were less than five minutes away. A better man might have resisted a little more, but Jonas never once claimed to be a good man.

He found a path and pulled to the side of the road, turning into the trees and parking. "It won't hide us too well if someone happens to be looking."

Taylor unclipped her seatbelt, her voice throaty. "It's

good enough for me." She reached for him, her hands gripping his face as she pulled him to her.

Her lips.

Jonas hadn't tasted them, hadn't felt them, in such a long time. God, he'd forgotten how good she tasted. He'd forgotten how soft her mouth was, and now that he had it, he almost didn't know what to do with himself.

So he held her. As though his body was finally coming alive after almost two years of being frozen stiff, Jonas grabbed Taylor by the waist, his other hand coming to rest on her back right before he pulled her to him.

Taylor's dark hair with those unbelievable blue high-lights fell into his face. It wasn't tied back anymore. When did that happen? Didn't matter, because then her arms were looping around his neck and it was so beyond perfect that he didn't know what to do with himself.

The heat and clench of her thighs around his legs, her perfect breasts pressed against his chest, and the way she leaned into his mouth...God, he missed this. He had missed her. So damned much it ached.

And now her tongue was in his mouth.

Taylor had always been a little on the aggressive side—came with being a bear shifter, Jonas had always assumed —but this was more than he anticipated. She kissed him as though she thought he was going to vanish if she stopped. Her nimble fingers worked quickly to undo the buttons of his shirt before she slid her hands against his bare chest, then down to his abdomen.

Jonas groaned, his body pushing up to meet her, his cock jumping to attention but still stuck behind his jeans.

Everywhere she touched him throbbed. Her fingers

left behind a trail of fire that made Jonas gasp for breath. Only she could touch him in a way that made him feel as though he'd never been touched. Only she could make his body come alive like this.

How the hell had he gone for so long without her? How did he ever manage to trick himself into thinking he didn't need her anymore? That he was over her? There was no getting over her, and there was no getting over this.

Jonas pulled her waist forward and back, grinding her down onto his erection while giving her a little preview of what was to come. Her small groan of approval was more than he needed to know he was on the right track.

"I forgot."

Jonas blinked his eyes open. "Sorry, what?"

She smiled at him, her full lips darker after being kissed. "I almost forgot what this felt like. I missed you so much."

Her fingers threaded into Jonas' hair, and something in his chest clenched painfully tight. He couldn't take this anymore. He really couldn't. "Come here." He gripped her hair tight enough that it had to hurt, but Taylor gave him no indication she was uncomfortable or in pain as she opened for him, letting his tongue slide forward to lick deep inside, as though their mouths were saying hello to each other after a long time spent apart.

The desperation and need vibrated from both of their bodies. Even with his spacious truck, there was no getting around the fact that dry humping each other on the driver's side made things a little cramped.

Without taking his mouth from Taylor's, Jonas

reached his hand down, fumbling for the handle to push the seat back.

His horn blared as Taylor pushed herself up onto her knees to give him space, and then the seat finally pushed back enough to provide them with the room they needed.

And nearly made them head-butt each other.

Taylor laughed. The first real laugh he'd heard out of her since he'd gotten here. She didn't stop touching him. Her eyes danced, and Jonas swore he'd never seen anyone more beautiful in his entire life.

"Taylor—"

She kissed his mouth before he could finish, but it was a quick kiss. She pulled back before he could get a handle on himself. "Don't say anything. Not right now. I don't want to ruin this."

"I won't ruin it."

It could never be ruined so long as she was here with him.

Apparently, Taylor didn't trust him not to ruin the mood with whatever she thought he was about to say because she kissed him again. Her mouth was perfection, so how could he resist her when she was like this?

They didn't remove their clothes so much as they just loosened them, getting to all the good parts that were needed the most to do what they wanted to do to each other.

"I wish I wore a skirt today," Taylor said with that wicked smile on her face, the sort of smile that brought Jonas back to the old days when they were together, and there was almost nothing in the world that could ruin the mood between them. Just the two of them against the world.

Taylor had to lift herself entirely off of Jonas' waist to get her jeans down, and holy hell, this was happening. Jonas quickly rummaged through this glove compartment, searching for just what he needed.

Taylor smiled, taking one of the little packets in her hands and tearing open the plastic, pulling out the latex with a shocking amount of skill.

"Should I be worried that you know how to do that so well?" Jonas could barely take his eyes off her fingers as she held his cock in her skillful hands, rolling the condom down his shaft.

"Should I be worried that you have a box of these in your truck?"

He cleared his throat. "No. I wouldn't think so, no."

She chuckled, that same laugh she used to give him whenever she got the better of him in one way or another. Then she was climbing onto his lap and settling onto his cock.

Jonas hissed low in his throat, gripping her waist and clenching his teeth as the sweet heat of her body, the clench of her sex, engulfed him.

And Taylor was clearly trying to drive him insane by the way she closed her eyes, parted her perfectly puckered lips as she sank inch by sweet inch down onto him. Then she was seated, and Jonas needed a minute to breathe before he could collect himself.

Taylor did, too.

"That feels…" She opened her eyes. "Exactly as I remember it."

Something wild and instinctive rose up and roared inside of Jonas' chest. He knew what she meant because he felt it, too, and even though Jonas was not a shifter, not for the first time, he felt a wild inner side sit up straight. Something animalistic and fierce.

And he wasn't about to hold it back either.

"Let it out," Taylor gasped, already canting her hips back and forth, riding him as though she'd never stopped. "Let me see it."

Jonas growled. "See what?"

She leaned in, her eyes glowing with the eager lust. He could see her inner bear ready to come out. "Let me see it."

Again, he didn't know what she meant, but part of him thought he understood. She was demanding something he didn't have. She wanted to see that wild shifter side to him — a side he didn't have.

But as a subhuman, there was a hint of something, something she could work with. Something she could see, and maybe he felt it, too.

Jonas gripped her hips tightly, encouraging the movement of her body, making her dance for him.

Taylor leaned forward, her face coming close to his chest. He thought she was about to kiss him there. Jonas wasn't entirely sure why, but he was willing to go with it.

Until Taylor pulled the lever that had Jonas falling backward.

No, she just let the seat lean back until it couldn't go any farther, and she laughed again at the look on his face. "You should see yourself right now."

"You should talk, sweetheart."

He didn't want to give Taylor the chance to make fun of him again, so he grabbed her by the back of her head and yanked her mouth down for another beautiful kiss.

He bit her lips sweetly, coaxing them open so he could taste her tongue the way he wanted to.

"You look like sex on wheels right now."

Taylor wet her lips. "I better, considering we're having sex right now."

She bit down on her lower lip after that, throwing her head back, and as she moaned, the sound, the vibration of her body, rocked through him. He could understand her need to push the seat back. It gave her all the room she needed to rock his world, and when it came to Taylor, she loved being on top. When she put him into this position, he was more than willing to let her do whatever she wanted.

The only thing he needed to do to keep up the momentum was to thrust his hips up, making her practically bounce on his cock. Jonas had to take some care with this, however. He didn't want Taylor bonking her head while he bonked her.

"I'm close," she rasped, circling her hips in the way she always did when her orgasm was just around the corner.

"Come for me, baby. I want to feel it."

"Are you close?"

Not quite yet, but he was going to get there one way or the other, and Jonas wasn't about to let her worry too much about it.

He reached for her breasts, still behind that sexy, blue lace bra. There was little in the world Jonas loved more than seeing her perfect pair of breasts behind a bra like that. It was almost a shame to undo it, but he needed to get his hands where they had to go.

Her nipples freed, Jonas took one of her perfect

breasts in his hand before he leaned in, kissing one of those caramel-colored nubs.

Taylor sighed. "Don't stop doing that."

"Doing this?" He pressed his teeth to her bud, enjoying the shiver that rippled through her body, and the way her sex clenched around his shaft.

"Y-yeah, just like that."

"Then show me." He kissed her other nipple, teasing it while his other hand slid down to her sex. To the curls of hair between her legs that he loved so much.

Too many women waxed absolutely everything off nowadays. He didn't like that. Taylor kept herself groomed, and as he could see, and feel, that hadn't changed. He pressed his fingers to her sex, stroking her, enjoying the feel of scratchy soft hair as Taylor rode him.

"Like this?"

"Yes."

She looped her arm back around his neck, gripping him tight as she rode him, and she was almost there. He could feel it as her pace increased right before Taylor sighed, her body shuddering, and Jonas felt a clenching and unclenching around his cock as she came.

Taylor came, sighing his name. Jonas was going to hold that one over her head for a little while. How could he not as she moved the way she did? As she fucked against him until she had nothing left to give.

"You're not done," Jonas growled, grabbing her by the hair and yanking her head back so he could look into those glowing golden eyes, seeing her wicked smile return after her moment of bliss. He crushed his mouth to hers once more, thrusting up into her, savoring the sounds of her moans as she rode him again. He knew she loved the control that came with the sex they had, especially when he was the one on the cusp of orgasm. She had him right where she wanted him.

Luckily for Jonas, he wasn't too far behind her, so there wasn't much of a chance for Taylor to sex torture him.

Next time. He would lay himself down to whatever tortures she had in mind for him.

"Not yet, don't come yet."

Jonas laughed a low, breathy noise. "D-don't exactly have a say in that right now, sweetheart."

Taylor nodded, her mouth quirking in a sexy, mischievous smile as she focused on the movement of her hips.

"All right. Come on then."

Jonas hissed, his toes curling in his boots as Taylor rode him.

So close. He was damn near there. Just a little bit more and...

Jonas came with a shout, wrapping his arms around Taylor's waist and clutching her tight.

Jonas wished he didn't have the condom on. He wanted to fuck her and claim her the way a real shifter did. Even if he was a subhuman, and even if it didn't necessarily mean the same thing. He wanted it. He wanted her to go back home and for Andrew everyone else who might have told her to turn her back on him to smell his scent all over her.

As he came down off the high of his orgasm, as the crash finished with him, Jonas realized he wanted Taylor for his mate. He wanted her for his wife. This was the mother of his child, and he wanted to spend the rest of his life with her.

He felt her soft stroke on his hair and back, and he pressed his ear to her chest to hear the sound of her beating heart as it calmed. For the first time in years, Jonas felt at peace.

Until he opened his eyes, looked out the front windshield of his truck, and spotted two wolves and a man, staring right at him and Taylor.

CHAPTER 14

Taylor didn't understand why Jonas suddenly stopped moving. When she looked back to see what he had his eyes on, she understood.

She jumped off him and into the passenger seat, pulling on her clothes, trying to keep her eyes on the wolves and the person they were with.

Something flicked. Long ears. She finally noted them, on top of the man's head. A shifter then. Those weren't wolf ears. He scratched at the back of his neck, looking away as color flooded his cheeks.

"Jesus Christ, how much of that were they watching?"

A dangerous growl, a terrible noise that could have belonged to an alpha, rumbled its way out of Jonas' throat. "I'll find out."

"What? Hey, wait!"

Taylor tried to grab for Jonas when she realized what he was doing. Jonas managed to fix his clothes and push his way out of the truck before she could stop him.

He might be subhuman, but he was no match for two wolves, and whatever that guy out there was.

"Stay in the truck! Lock the doors!"

Uh, yeah right. That wasn't about to happen. Much as Taylor occasionally liked letting men pretend at being all protective and possessive, when it came to her and Jonas, she was the one with the claws around here.

Jonas gave her a hard look when she didn't get back into the truck. She flipped him off. She had her own bone to pick with people who watched a woman having sex without her knowing.

"What the hell did you think you were doing?"

"Taylor—"

"What kind of asshole goes around watching someone like that?"

"Sorry, sorry," said the man, raising his hands. He refused to look at her, as if that was going to help her out now. "I wasn't trying…We followed your truck after you left the station and found you here. We weren't watching."

"Bullshit," Jonas growled. "You were standing right there! What the hell is your problem?"

"Whoa, okay, hold up a minute."

It was interesting how the two wolves did nothing while Jonas approached the shifter in the middle. They just watched as the guy stumbled and backed away, as though he feared he was about to get the crap beaten out of him.

Which looked like it might be the case.

"Steve! Jackson! Will you help me already?"

Jonas snatched the man by the throat, yanking him close enough that their noses practically touched.

"You're lucky I don't have my ax on me, you little shithead, or I'd shove it so far up your ass you'd—"

"Jonas!"

They shifted so fast, and Taylor was so distracted by the chest pounding display that she was late warning him when one of the wolves transformed. The biggest of the two slammed his hand onto Jonas' shoulder. "That's enough. Let him go."

"You don't have to hurt him to make your point. He didn't want to be here in the first place," the second chimed in.

Taylor was so done with this. She let her claws out, a protective instinct whirling within her as the wolf shifters surrounded her man. She made sure the bald guy knew she was coming, however. She didn't want anyone to spin around with their fist ready and catch her off guard. "You'd both better step back right now, or else someone might get hurt. It won't be me, and it won't be him either."

All four men slowly turned to look at her, as though the sound of her threatening voice was somehow a shock to them. Not that she understood what that was about. They didn't have to look at her as if they didn't understand where this was coming from.

Jonas especially, the asshole. She was trying to save him.

The man Jonas held by the throat smiled nervously at her. The other two just stared. Jonas raised his brows, and she could feel the sudden increase of heat in his body.

The bald man turned his attention back to Jonas. "If you would release our friend here, I would like to be able to speak with the both of you before your mate decides to attack us."

"If she did attack, you would all deserve to get ripped

apart. I sure as shit wouldn't stop her."

The man Jonas held sputtered. "We just wanted to see you. Th-that was my sister at the fire station. My sister and her mate. We're not here to cause trouble."

"Your sister?" Taylor thought about that, looking at the man's tail. It did look like a fox tail, and so did his ears. It didn't prove they were related, but why would he lie about something like that? The idea that he was worried about his sister did give her pause, and a feeling of sympathy, even though she didn't have siblings of her own.

If Meg ever had siblings, then Taylor would want other people to give her consideration if she ever had to look out for them.

It didn't make any sense, but maybe it didn't need to. Taylor already knew what she wanted.

"Jonas, you think you could let up a little?"

His brows raised high again. "Seriously?"

Taylor let her claws sink back into her fingernails, the itch of fur retracting into her pores tingling across her skin. "I want to hear them out."

Jonas growled, turning that horrible stare back to the man in his hand before he shoved the guy away.

The fox stumbled, caught himself, then rubbed at his throat while glaring at Jonas.

Jonas pointed a thick finger at him. "Don't even think about giving me shit for that. You were the one perving on my mate."

Taylor's heart twisted. She pressed her lips together quickly, trying not to keep her gaze on Jonas for too long.

Was he aware of what he just said?

If that word came to him so quickly, then it meant—

"We just wanted to talk. We want the same thing," said

the bald wolf shifter, holding out his hand. "My name is Jackson."

Jonas eyed the hand suspiciously, but then reached out and took it. "You got a last name?"

Jackson grinned. "Dwayne."

"Wait, that's your last name?" said the other shifter, staring at him with amazement.

"There a problem?" Jackson asked, not entirely giving the other man a dirty look, but it wasn't so easygoing either.

"No, I just figured you had something a little different. You know? It doesn't exactly suit you."

Jackson growled, and Taylor was getting sick of this entire thing. "Would you boys just hurry up and tell us why you were watching me and Jonas in the truck? You're giving off serial killer vibes."

Jonas growled at the fox guy again, who took a few more steps backward.

"We're not here to hurt you, and we didn't watch you," said the other wolf. "My name is Steve Delany. I work as a private eye in Astraea. We followed you here and stopped in front of the truck when we wanted to get your attention. We didn't know what you were doing."

Jonas didn't sound too impressed by the explanation, which was good. Taylor wanted to stay angry with these guys, and if she was going to do that, then she wanted Jonas to have her back.

"What we were doing and where we were doing it is not your damned business," Jonas snapped. "What's a private eye doing in Lakeview? The fires here would be outside of your expertise."

"Nothing is outside of my expertise," Steve said, his

tone a little too cocky for Taylor.

She cracked her knuckles, reminding the boys she was there and letting her claws return just enough to be noticeable. "So what do you all want?" This had better be good, too. She didn't just have the afterglow of the best sex she'd had in months interrupted because a group of shifters wanted to have a chat. "You said this was about your sister?" She looked to the fox. "You still didn't introduce yourself."

"Right." The guy was still bright red around his neck and cheeks, but Taylor was way too miffed to show him any pity. "My name is Link Wolff, and my sister, Zelda… she used to be married into the pack we think is doing all of this. The paramedics you called saved my brother-in-law's life. We…I owe you for that."

Taylor blinked, such an honest, open answer catching her off guard. "Oh, well…you're welcome."

Link nodded.

Jonas narrowed his eyes. "Your name is Link?"

Link's entire body clenched up, the picture of a male readying himself for a fight. "Yeah?"

"And your sister's name is Zelda?"

For a hair of a second, Taylor didn't get it, but then she did. She didn't even like video games, but the reference wasn't lost on her. And now she was back to staring at the guy, and his two friends, with massive suspicion. "You're telling me that's your name? Your legal name? For you and your sister?"

Link rolled his eyes. "My parents were freaks, all right? Will you just let us talk to you, please?" Even as he said it, Link still seemed to have trouble looking at her.

Whatever.

"What do you think, Jonas?"

Jonas still didn't look happy. He looked like he wanted to throw down and take out all three shifters right here and now, but he sighed and relented. "All right, fine. What do you know about these wolves?"

Steve nodded. "Right, well, for one thing, they are a murderous bunch, and if they're starting fires like this, then they're even dumber than we all thought."

"Arsonists usually are," Jonas agreed. "Tell me something I don't know."

"The conduit is my mate." Jonas and Taylor stared at Steve while he continued to explain that his best friend was Zelda's mate and that his meeting with the conduit had set the war with the wolves in motion and gotten them all involved.

Jackson spoke next, and his words chilled Taylor to the bone. "We think someone in her bear sloth is helping the wolves set the fires."

Taylor caught her breath as her blood ran cold and pieces fell into place in her mind. Without a word, she turned and ran for the truck, which still had the keys in the ignition.

"Taylor, wait!"

She didn't wait. She jumped into the driver's seat and started the ignition. Jonas barely got into the passenger seat before she was on the move.

"Jesus! Taylor! Wait for just a second! We don't even know if what he said is true."

She shook her head. "I don't care. I left my baby back home."

And she wasn't going to stop until she had Meg safely in her arms.

Jonas barely held on for the ride or got his door shut, as Taylor sped down the highway well over the speed limit. She turned onto the road that led to her territory, and Jonas knew he had to think fast.

"Taylor, you need to think rationally about this."

She shook her head, and it was a miracle she was able to drive as well as she did with that wild expression in her eyes.

"If you go storming back home looking like that, and if what those guys said was true, you could give everything away."

"I'm not taking the risk. I want her back. I need her back."

"I do, too, but—"

"You're not acting like it!" Taylor slammed her hand onto the steering wheel, turning that enraged expression onto him before looking back at the road. "We left her there, and she might be in trouble!"

"Of course I do! I would have cared a long time ago if you'd bothered to tell me she existed!" It just came out. He still had anger and hurt about it, but should have kept it inside. The swell of moisture in Taylor's eyes showed that it was too much to think about past mistakes while frantically trying to get to Meg right then.

He focused, bringing calm back into himself. He was no good to anyone, not even Taylor or Meg if he couldn't keep his head. One of them had to. He put his hand onto Taylor's. "Baby, pull over. Please. We've got maybe one chance at this."

Her hand shook. He felt the tickle of hairs under his fingers and palm as she struggled to keep her inner bear in check. She let out a shaky breath before slowing the truck down and guiding it over to the side of the road.

She wouldn't stop trembling. He'd never seen her like this before, and it stunned him. And he wanted to ease her out of that pain. Everything inside him drew him to her. She was a magnet, and he was stuck in her pull. Almost two years away and he'd thought he was over her. He thought there was nothing left between them and now he couldn't yank himself away from her even if he wanted to.

"Baby, nothing is going to happen to Meg."

"Then we need to get home before something does happen."

"I know, and we will, but if what those men said was true and you rush in there looking ready for a fight, it will put them on the defensive and cause them to act. You need to stay calm. All right? If Andrew has anything to do with this—"

"You think he's involved?"

Shit. "No, not necessarily, but maybe he's close to

someone who is. The point is that you can't give us away to anyone when we get back. All right? Not yet. Wait until you have Meg safely in your arms and then, when you're out of there, and at a safe distance, the police can get involved and start asking questions."

She looked at him. "Won't you be one of the men asking those questions."

"I've told you, I don't have any actual authority here. I was just here to help, not to carry out any real investigation."

As far as Jonas was concerned, he was done. He'd done his part, Dallas was still alive, and now the police could take over.

"Can we go home now?"

Jonas looked at her. She seemed to be in control again. There was still that edge of panic in her voice, the need to move quickly and get to her destination, but he supposed that was never going to entirely go away when it came to a mother worried about her baby.

"All right, but remember what I said. We have to be careful about this. As controlled as possible, so no one sniffs anything out about us. All right?"

Taylor put the truck back into drive, not looking at him as she nodded.

Jonas was pretty sure he was going to regret this, but he sat back and let her go, not saying another word until they were driving up the road and into the territory, houses and trailers coming into view.

"Remember what I said."

Her jaw tensed. She nodded as she drove right up to Andrew's deck, parking practically right in front of the wooden steps before hopping out of the truck. Jonas clenched his teeth, but he didn't say anything to her while he tried to ignore the sloth members who watched them from their houses. He decided not to look in any particular direction, knowing that any one of them, or even several of them, could be helping to set the fires.

But why? What purpose did the fire serve other than to terrorize a community? Was that the only point? Or was he looking for hidden layers that weren't there? He'd been in houses set aflame by people who loved their lighters a little too much. Sometimes, most of the time actually, there was no point. There was no big revenge plot. There was nothing other than the need to see something burn, to terrorize, and see things made clean by the fire. This could very well be that sort of case, but Jonas wasn't about to lower his guard or stop looking either.

Just in case.

Andrew stepped out of the front door, Meg in his arms, and the hairs on the back of Jonas' neck stood on end. He wanted to rush up there and yank his little girl from Andrew. He didn't trust anyone other than Taylor to hold her after what Steve, Jackson, and Link revealed on the side of the road.

And if this was what he felt, there was no telling how hard it was for Taylor to handle this.

"Made it back alright?"

"Yup." Taylor put on a mask that sure as hell would have had him fooled if he didn't know what was going on. She trotted up the stairs and reached for Meg, smiling as easily as though she was getting off from a day at the daycare and was eager to see her child again.

"Did you miss Mommy?"

"She was very good while you were away." Andrew

seemed a little too easygoing as he eased the child into Taylor's arms.

It was sweet the way Meg reached for her mother while sucking on her soother.

Then Andrew looked down at where she'd parked. "Ah, you miss the usual spot?"

"Sorry," Taylor said, smiling as though embarrassed about her parking capabilities. "It's been a long night. I was just a little eager to get home and see her. Right, baby?"

Meg smiled around her soother.

She didn't look like she was suffering from any trauma, but would a one-year-old baby, almost one-and-a-half, be able to pick up on that kind of vibe? Would she know it if she was in any danger?

Jonas couldn't be sure, and it didn't matter. The point was that he had Meg and Taylor here with him now and he was getting them out of here.

"Taylor, come on, we're going to be late."

"Right," she said, smiling at him with that wide-eyed, open expression, as if she knew what they were going to be late for. "You're right. Sorry. I'll just get her bag, and we'll be on our way."

"Where are you both off to?"

He said it so casually. The worst part about the tone of voice was the way Jonas couldn't tell if there was anything sinister about it. If anything was underlying in those words.

"I'm going to stay with Jonas for a bit." Even Jonas knew the best lies were the ones laced with a bit of truth. "He needs to get back to work, and I think it's a good idea to go to the city with him. Give him a chance to get to know Meg a little more."

He looked at that little girl, and he wanted to get to know her. He wanted to watch her grow up and protect her along the way. If Andrew had anything to do with the fires around here, or if he was covering for someone… Jonas wanted his daughter nowhere near him in that case.

Andrew shrugged, not giving any resistance to the plans he and Taylor gave. "All right, but you make sure to come and visit now, understand?"

Taylor blinked, giving the first little slip of her mask. "Really? Just like that?"

"Why not? You're a grown woman. You can do whatever you want."

Jonas didn't want to risk that this was a trap, or that this might not be what he thought, or hoped that it was. "Taylor, come on. Let's go and get Meg's things." He didn't want to take the time to get the damned baby bag. They could easily get more supplies in the city, but it would look suspicious if they rushed out too fast.

Taylor nodded, heading down the stairs, "I'll contact the parents and let them know the daycare will be shuttered for a while."

"Good luck," Andrew called after them.

Jonas settled his arm around Taylor's waist, walking away with her, back to her trailer so he could grab some things.

A few men stepped in his way. Black bears he'd known from his days living just outside the sloth. "Guys, we're in a bit of a hurry."

"Right," said the man in the middle, narrowing his eyes at Jonas. Trevor always was a sack of shit. He was skinnier than Jonas was, and not that tall, but he knew he could outmatch him because of his abilities, which he'd liked throwing around when they were kids.

"Did you guys go to the police?"

"What? No, of course not."

Taylor spoke a little too quickly for Jonas' liking. Even he could hear the lie in her voice, and he was the one who wanted to give her the most leeway right about now.

Trevor didn't look too impressed. He crossed his arms, as if he was trying to make himself look bigger, which was next to impossible considering his size. "You sure about that? Because you were gone a long time."

Jonas clenched his hands behind Taylor's back. "Why? Did you have a visitor?"

Trevor glared at him. Jonas glared right back.

"You remember that I can kick your ass, right?"

Trevor's lackeys had to grab his shoulders and yank him back before he could get anywhere. Jonas knew better than to think age had made these guys mature out of picking any fight they could. No. They stopped because Andrew was still standing on his deck, watching them.

Trevor looked up at Jonas, then shook his head. "You're lucky boss man is watching you right now, or you would be dead in the water."

"Why? Are you hiding something?"

"Jonas, let's just go." Taylor grabbed him by his sleeve, trying to pull him away from the confrontation.

His feet felt as if they were weighed down with irons. He didn't want to move, but ultimately, he did. He had to. This was not the time for a fight even if there was a chance he could win it. Which there wasn't.

He couldn't fight when there was a baby to think

about, and he needed to get Taylor out of here before they drew too much of a crowd. As he passed Trevor, he noticed some marks on his arms looked like the tell-tale signs of a run-in with the wolves at one point. Jonas wondered if the wolves could be threatening Trevor if he didn't help them. Even dickheads like Trevor still had family to protect. People to watch out for.

He and Taylor rushed inside her trailer. Jonas locked the door behind him, but he knew that wouldn't stop a shifter who wanted to get in.

"You think they know?" Taylor asked, her voice low, a little scared even.

Jonas put his finger to his mouth. He wasn't about to take the risk that someone was listening in on them.

Taylor nodded and immediately rushed into action, packing clothes, blankets, diapers, packets of baby food, wipes, powders, and an assortment of other things Jonas wasn't sure if they needed at that moment, but what did he know about caring for a baby?

"Are you ready?"

"Almost." Taylor grabbed something else out of the crib—a Piglet doll, and stuffed it into her bag. Jonas took the bag from her and slung it around his shoulder before the three of them were out the door.

Where they were immediately stopped by the number of people standing between them and the truck.

CHAPTER 16

If Taylor had been a cat shifter, she was pretty sure her hackles would have gone up. If her daughter wasn't in her arms, there was no way in hell she would have been able to keep her head about her as Trevor, Andrew, and the entire Council of Elders stood in a circle around her door.

Meg groaned, as though she was picking up on the strange frequency around her and didn't like it.

"It's okay, baby. Momma's here," and she wasn't about to let a damned thing happen to her daughter.

Jonas dropped the bag, taking a step forward. "Hey, guys. What's going on?"

Taylor looked to Andrew. He looked sorry. He pressed his lips together, but he at least had the decency to look her in the eyes while he betrayed her.

"Andrew?"

Andrew shook his head. "I'm sorry, sweetie. I didn't know about this until this morning."

"Horse shit," Jonas snapped, his shoulders bunching.

"Are you fucking kidding me? Are there even any wolves involved in those fires at all?"

"There are," Trevor said, nodding. "And they're going to come here and burn everything down if we don't play nice."

"What does play nice mean?" Taylor asked. "Does it mean I can't take my little girl out of here?"

"None of us can take our little girls out of here," Trevor snapped, glaring at her. "You're not special."

Taylor grit her teeth at that.

No, she wasn't special, and logically she knew her daughter wasn't any better than the young kids who lived and played here either, but if given a choice…

She would still want to take Meg and leave here and damn all the consequences.

Apparently, all it took for Taylor to realize she was a terrible, selfish person was to have a kid of her own, and to realize what she was willing to do for her offspring.

"None of you have to stay here and put up with this. None of you have to be terrorized," Jonas said.

"That's simple for you to say," said one of the elders. Taylor noted the way the older man's hand clenched tightly around the cane he held. Thick knuckles white around the wood as he glared at Jonas. "You're not one of us. You don't have any connections to the land or desire to fight for what's yours."

Taylor winced at that, noting the clench in Jonas' jaw.

"You think that, do you?"

He wouldn't fight an old man, would he? An elderly shifter was probably one of the few shifters Jonas had a chance at besting in a fight.

Though that didn't mean he was set to win, much as Taylor hated to admit that.

"Jonas," Taylor put her hand on his arm, stunned when he yanked away from her.

"Many of you have children here. Just go to the damned police! Trevor! Describe the people who did that to you. You can help put these bastards away and get this over with before someone gets hurt."

"Someone was hurt, you prick! Me! And that fire near the entrance of our sloth? That was a warning, so was the fire up there!" Trevor pointed a long finger up the mountain where smoke still blackened the sky.

Jonas didn't seem impressed. "So what do they want from you? For you to help them get the conduit?"

Taylor tried not to look at him when he mentioned the C word. She didn't want anyone around her knowing she'd met with the people the wolves were searching for. That she might know a little more than she was letting on. It would only spell disaster for her, Meg, and Jonas.

"I know you met up with outsiders. Two wolves and a fox? I heard the whole damned thing."

Taylor sucked back a heavy gasp. She backed up a step, though she felt as though she'd been punched.

Trevor was always known for getting around, for being in places he wasn't supposed to be. For being stealthy and sneaky. It was his best-damned trait. She should have known. She should have seen this coming a mile away. Of course, he could overhear something she didn't want him hearing.

Jonas stepped in front of her, blocking off Trevor's view. It didn't help. Taylor still felt cold all over. Her gaze fell to Andrew. This time, Andrew wouldn't look at her.

No. No. This couldn't be happening.

The head elder spoke. "We need to know where the conduit is."

"Ask Trevor," Jonas snapped. "I'm done here."

"You will go nowhere."

All the elders put their hands up, mirroring the actions of the head elder.

That chill deepened in Taylor's gut.

She'd always thought of these people as being helpers for the sloth. They were here to administer advice on marriage and vegetable gardens and help the alpha handle unruly cubs whose parents weren't all that involved.

Seeing them as they were now, as one unit, gave Taylor an idea of how powerful they really were. These weren't the people who convinced her to walk away from Jonas when he wanted to leave for the city. These weren't just well-meaning elderly shifters that the younger generations looked up to because of their age and wisdom. They had real power in the sloth, and Andrew seemed powerless to do or say anything against them.

Or he was unwilling to say anything against them. Taylor couldn't decide which was worse.

"You're going to help hand over an innocent woman to a pack of murderous wolves? To save yourselves?" she asked.

Andrew closed his eyes. "It's not just me, Taylor. Look at everyone else around here. You're not the only one with a baby to think of."

She flinched at that, and was too much of a coward to look around when Andrew gestured to the rest of the sloth.

The elders weren't having it. "Look at us!"

She jumped, then did as she was told almost against her own will.

She looked around at Trevor, the elders, Andrew, and the other bears who had come to stand around and see what the fuss was about. Some looked on as though they were as shocked to learn all of this as Taylor was. Others seemed resigned, but the one thing that stood out was the cubs in attendance. Toddlers, a few of the younger cubs who came to her daycare from time to time. The older kids, and then the teenagers.

Taylor had wanted to think only about Meg, but these sloth cubs were her family too. She couldn't leave it all behind like Jonas could, she owed her sloth and these kids more than that. Having to look at them put her to shame.

Jonas wasn't having it. "That's enough. She gets the point."

"You were going to leave us, too."

Jonas narrowed his eyes at everyone surrounding them. "I was never part of the sloth, remember? There was nothing for me to leave behind."

"Don't be stupid," Trevor snapped, but then followed up with nothing else.

Taylor was too upset with herself, with everything around her, to even look too much into what Jonas had just said. To wonder if he'd feel the same way if she hadn't agreed to leave with him. Were her and Meg something to leave behind? Either way, it wasn't the time for her to get hung up on petty insecurities.

"Andrew," Taylor called out to him. At first, she thought he was going to avoid looking at her, but eventually, he met her gaze. "Andrew, don't do this."

"It's my job to watch out for our people."

"By keeping them from leaving? Keeping them prisoners here?" Jonas asked. "You were the one who got up and told everyone that you cared about their safety."

"I do."

"You said you cared about Taylor and Meg. You supported her choices before, but when she chooses to take her baby and leave with me, that's where you draw your line?"

Taylor couldn't stand the fighting. Everything felt too personal, too close to breaking out into something that could get violent. There was a time when she would have jumped into any fight with the boys, but that was long ago. Holding a baby in her arms, her baby, had changed all that.

Now she looked to the elders, to the people charged with guiding the bears who lived here, and they stared back at her with the same knowing expressions they always did.

As if they knew better and thought it would be just a matter of time before she could see it their way.

Taylor didn't want to see it their way. She wanted to get out of here. To leave this place with her baby and the father of that child.

"Andrew, I never told you this, but you've helped me out so much over the last two and half years. Longer than that. You've been like a father to me at times, and I've always...I loved and respected you like a father, too. Please, please, I want to go with Jonas. I don't want this for Meg. I don't want to risk being here when fires are being set like this. If the other parents feel the same way, let them leave too. If it's not safe, then let us go."

Something changed in Andrew's eyes. His chest puffed

out as he inhaled a deep breath through his nose, but then he deflated when he glanced towards the elders. They clearly had their hooks that deeply into him.

Or maybe he'd never had control to begin with. Maybe they'd only let him, and the sloth, think he had.

"Taylor, nothing will happen to you or Meg. I swear. I will personally make sure of that. All right?"

Now she wanted to cry. Her image of her alpha and her sloth was being shattered. The life she'd invested in, to the point of spending years away from Jonas, was crumbling around her.

"All we have to do is mind our own business. Stay here, don't pay attention to any of the wolves or the conduit stuff. They'll leave us alone," Andrew said.

Taylor shook her head. She couldn't look at him anymore. She didn't see her friend. She didn't see the man who let her cry on his shoulder. She saw a stranger, and she couldn't process that.

"And if we don't agree to that?" Jonas asked. "Because you're all out of your damned minds if you think any of you are getting near Taylor."

Her heart did a painful twist. Even after all of this, after staring down an entire sloth full of angry bears, he was still willing to put himself between her and danger.

"We just want you to sit back and relax for a little," Andrew said. "Don't go into anything irrationally. We can work this out."

"How?" Jonas demanded.

Trevor sneered, liking this a little too much. "How about you get the fuck back inside and stop talking? You're not in charge here, asshole."

"Neither are you, shithead," Taylor snapped.

"Shit," Meg said, and any other time, Taylor might have wanted to curl into a ball of humiliation and die for that, but as she was being shoved back inside the door to her home, all she could think about was how she was going to get her little girl out of this.

CHAPTER 17

Jonas had to remind himself again and again that he was just a subhuman. He was stronger than most humans without any gym time, and he could damn near hold onto the hose by himself without a second man to steady him, but much as Trevor's face was begging to be punched in, Jonas wouldn't last too long against him.

He had to take it easy. He let Trevor search him and take his phone, growling at the man when he went to do the same to Taylor.

Andrew was nothing but apologetic to Taylor, as if that somehow changed anything. She seemed to have enough of this garbage, though.

"Andrew, it smells like burning wood the second you walk outside. You want me to stay here?"

"I don't have a choice, sweetheart."

"Stop calling me that!"

Meg let out an anguished wail. Even if she weren't a little shifter, it would be next to impossible not pick up on her mother's emotions like this. She knew something was wrong, but the poor kid didn't know what, and Jonas' heart ached for her while Taylor yelled at Andrew.

And, pathetic coward that he was, Andrew stood there and took it.

Jonas was half tempted to take Meg from Taylor's arms so she could really unload on Andrew. He got the feeling that if Taylor tried attacking him, then Andrew would do little to defend himself.

That would be amazing to watch.

"Bet you think you're gonna do something right now, don't 'cha?"

Jonas ignored Trevor. The little peckerhead was still trying his damnedest to bring some reaction out of Jonas. A reaction he was not willing to give the other man.

"Come on, you can admit it. You're looking at Andrew like you want to go ape shit on him."

"Nope, not working, Trevor."

"Sure it is." Trevor pointed a dirty finger less than an inch from Jonas' nose. "I can see it all over you. I'm getting under your skin."

"Wasn't talking about that." Jonas couldn't resist. "I was talking about how your daddy still isn't proud of you."

He should have resisted harder, because the fist that caught Jonas in the gut caught him off guard, even when he saw it coming.

The air whooshed out of his lungs. He couldn't even make out the things Trevor was yelling at him because Jonas was too busy trying not to puke all over Taylor's floor as he coughed and sucked back every sip of fresh air he could get.

He could hear Meg crying, and Taylor yelling. Andrew

shouted something. Jonas tried to push himself to his feet, if only to stop the bastard from taking his worthless aggression out on her, but then a strong hand pressed down on his shoulder, keeping Jonas on his knees.

He didn't have the strength to get back up, and his vision only just stopped tunneling, so he didn't want to take the risk of anything else happening to Meg if he fought back.

Eventually, Andrew pushed Trevor out the front door. He seemed to be yelling at the other man the entire time, as if he was angry with him. Maybe he was, but Jonas liked it so much more when Taylor slammed the door behind the both of them and locked it when they were out.

Meg was still crying, but she was safe in her mother's arms as Taylor came back to him, kneeling and checking on him while he coughed up the last of his pride.

"Are you all right?"

"Yeah," Jonas said, feeling very much as though he was choking on those words. He was a little, but he was more embarrassed than anything. "Sorry."

"Don't be. Jesus, he could have broken your ribs."

Jonas didn't want to hear about how fragile he was when he tried to protect Taylor and Meg from all of this. He pushed himself to his feet, ignoring the screaming pull in his stomach as he stretched out those muscles.

"Are you all right to stand?"

Jonas cleared his throat, rubbing at his stomach. "I'll be good. He just sucker punched me is all."

Jonas also knew he was going to have a nasty, bear-shaped bruise on his abdomen by tomorrow morning, and he was going to be in a lot more pain then, so he had to hurry up and get through this before everything went to complete shit.

"We have to get you out of here." Much as Jonas hated that his little girl was crying like this, at least her cries gave cover to everything else he was saying. If Trevor or anyone else happened to be listening with their ears to the outside walls, hoping to catch Jonas and Taylor plotting their escape, then a baby crying was a plausible excuse rather than a TV turned up too high.

Taylor rocked her daughter, but it didn't seem to do much to help as Meg wailed.

He touched her back, wishing he could do something, even if the cries were useful.

The cries continued.

"How are we supposed to leave when they took our phones? My laptop?"

"Do you have anything else in the house? A landline they might've forgotten about?"

Taylor shook her head, the helplessness in her eyes, in the air around her as she tried to comfort her daughter, came through hard. Taylor's eyes swam. She rubbed at her forehead and looked around her own home as though she couldn't understand how it came to be this way, how she'd become trapped here.

Jonas pressed his hands to her shoulders. "I'll figure this out."

Taylor yanked herself away from him. "How? How are you going to get Meg and me out of here? We didn't even...I didn't see this coming. How could I not see this coming?"

"It's not your fault."

"It is my fault! You told me so many times that I

needed to go to the police. You told me this would…you said…"

"And you did go. You went to the police with me. You gave your statement; that was all I asked you to do."

Taylor didn't seem to be hearing him. He grabbed her shoulders again, holding on tight. He had no intention of ever letting this woman go. This was the mother of his child. His mate. He turned his back on her once, and he was never going to do that again.

"Taylor, look at me. Hey, look at me."

She did. Her eyes glowed a golden brown, showing how close she was to losing all control.

"We're going to get out of this. So is Meg. All three of us. We're fine. You hear me?"

"How are we fine? We're stuck in here, and Andrew went crazy, and he's letting the elders walk all over him like he thinks they're in charge."

Jonas knew what she meant. Elders were supposed to have some weight in a pack or clan, sloth or skulk, but they weren't the ones who ran things. Everyone knew that. Even the humans. Something else was happening here.

"Maybe they made a deal with the wolves behind Andrew's back. Something could be making him do that, but come on, you know Andrew. He wouldn't hurt you, and I doubt he would ever want to hurt Meg."

At this point, Jonas wasn't entirely sure of that, but it was the only thing he had to work with to keep Taylor calm, so he was going to stick with that story.

"We'll figure out what this is, but we have to keep our heads clear and our eyes open. There's going to be a way out of this, and when we find it, we have to take it. Understand?"

Taylor didn't look as though she wanted to wait for anything to happen. She looked as though she wanted to take Meg and start running in a state of panic right now.

So Jonas was pleased when she inhaled a deep breath and reluctantly nodded. "All right."

Just by looking at her, Jonas could tell her heart was still hammering. He could see it in the fluttering pulse at the side of her throat. He could even hear it a little, and his hearing wasn't that good compared to a shifter's.

"I'll get you both through this. All right? I promise. I'll think of something."

Even now his mind raced, but Jonas couldn't think of much of anything that could be done. He knew people were watching Taylor's trailer. They were listening, hoping to hear something. And making sure they didn't go anywhere.

And that was the problem. Jonas wanted to bust his way out of here. He wanted to roar and pull forward all the strength he had to fight off everyone who would dare stop him and Taylor from leaving here when they wanted to. He was going to to take his mate and daughter to safety.

It wasn't much of a comfort that he knew he wouldn't be able to fight his way out of this situation even if he had been born a shifter. There were too many people to fight against.

If there hadn't been, Andrew might not have bothered going along with what the elders wanted.

The little round, black ears on top of Taylor's head twitched, her spine going suddenly going stiff.

"Do you hear that?"

At first, he didn't, but Jonas strained his ears and waited patiently for whatever it was that caught Taylor's attention to hit him.

Then it did.

Trucks. At least a couple of large vehicles. There were a few of them.

"Andrew expecting someone over?" Jonas marched to the window, pulling the curtain to the side just a crack so he could have a glance outside.

Two white trucks pulled up the dirt road leading out of the bears' territory. Jonas tried to get a look at the plates, but he couldn't make out anything from here. He just saw Andrew standing and waiting for them, and when the trucks stopped and parked in front of him, no less than four men got out.

All of them had wolf ears and tails.

"This is bad."

"What? What is it?" Taylor came to stand next to him, glancing out the window just as Andrew shook the hands of each man. What made it worse was when the elders approached to greet the wolves as well.

As if some sort of agreement had been come to.

"Oh my God. Oh my God, oh my God."

"Don't panic. We can still get out of this."

"How?"

Jonas had no idea, but he was going to think of something. "What else did Trevor and the others take before they left?"

"Uh…" Taylor seemed to struggle with that. "I think just the electronics. Why?"

Jonas hadn't seen anyone spend too much time in the

kitchen when they were setting up their kidnapping operation. One guy did walk away with Taylor's wooden block of knives, but Jonas hadn't seen anything else get taken.

He hoped it was because this had been overlooked and not because someone had already been in here before he and Taylor had tried to leave.

He yanked open the top drawer to the left of the sink, and then smiled at what he saw inside.

"They didn't take everything." He pulled out a long, mean-looking butcher knife.

Taylor stepped up beside him, keeping her voice a little quieter now that Meg was starting to tire herself out. "What are you going to do with that?"

"Hopefully nothing. Here, you take this one." She had other knives, including one that was hidden beneath the plastic separator for the forks and spoons. The knife he gave to her had a bright yellow handle, but it also had a matching plastic sheath for it.

That was good. If Jonas was going to give Taylor anything sharp while she had a baby in her arms then at least he could handle knowing there was some protection for Meg.

Taylor hesitated, but then took the knife.

"You'll only use it if you have to. I'll try to keep you out of a position where that's necessary."

Her throat worked in a swallow. "Do you think it will be necessary?"

He hoped not, but with everything going on here, he trusted these people about as much as he trusted a hungry dog next to a steak dinner.

Or a pyro-happy wolf next to a lighter.

"I don't want to hurt anyone, Jonas. This is my sloth. My family."

"She is your family," he whispered, pointing to Meg and wishing she would start crying again so he wouldn't have to hide the sound of his own voice. "If anyone tries anything with her, then your job is to protect her above everything and everyone else."

"Even you?"

He looked at her, his chest aching. "You know the answer to that question."

Taylor winced. Jonas hated to say that to her, but it had to be done. No amount of feeling between them was above the need they both had to protect Meg.

Unfortunately, he didn't get the chance to further prepare her for whatever else might be coming for them, because there was a noise at the door.

Someone was trying to open it, and realizing they couldn't.

Jonas always knew having a door lock while living in a pack of anything was a bit on the pointless side, especially when the door burst open and two of the wolf shifters who had stepped out of the truck, along with Trevor, stepped inside.

And Trevor smiled as though he was getting the best-damned present in the whole world.

Jonas stepped in front of Taylor.

Trevor nodded to them. "He's the one right there who got the police involved. Have at him if you want."

CHAPTER 18

Meg started to fuss again as the two wolf shifters came into Taylor's home, mucking it up with a stink that was unfamiliar to her.

Taylor quickly unsheathed her blade, but even then she knew she could only use it as a last resort. She could not fight while holding her child in her arms.

But she had to do something. The two shifters spread out, coming to either side of Jonas.

"You guys don't have to do anything. He's not going to go to anyone or say anything."

"He won't anymore," Trevor sang.

She snapped at him. "Will you shut the fuck up, you pathetic little weasel! No one likes you. No one will ever like you. Especially not your dead dad, so stop trying to act tough already!"

Trevor stepped forward. "You want to say shit to me again, you little—"

He stopped real fast when she pointed the knife at

him. "You take one more step towards me, and we'll see how brave you feel when I cut your ears off."

Trevor cursed.

"Yeah, you thought you were careful, did you? Stay the fuck away from me."

"Fuck," Meg said.

"That a girl."

Trevor looked to the two wolf shifters in the room with him. "Well? Aren't 'cha going to do something?"

They chuckled amongst themselves. "Deal with your bitch. Not our fault you can't handle her."

Taylor had never in her life seen the hairs on Trevor's ears bristle that hard, or his face turn that particular shade of red.

It was kind of scary, if she was honest.

She didn't even have to do the threatening after that. Jonas did. "Trevor, I know you're a sad sack of shit, but I swear to God, if you take one step towards her, I will do everything in my power to beat the living piss out of you. Do you understand me?"

"Fuck you, subhuman. You couldn't beat the piss out of my kid sister."

Taylor nearly did a double take. "You don't have a kid sister."

Trevor shrugged and looked at her as if she was ruining some great joke. "If I had one! All right? Christ."

Idiot. God, she couldn't believe she'd ever stood up for him.

She looked to the wolves distrustfully, hating them. "So what do you want? There are no conduits around here for you to rape and impregnate, so you can all go away."

The wolves looked amongst each other, then at her.

"You have the smell of the one who took the conduit from us on you. Tell us where they went and we'll let you go."

Taylor opened her mouth to tell them she had no idea where they went, but Jonas beat her to the answer.

"Her mate's name is Steve Delany; he's a private detective who works in Astraea, and he's got the entire police force behind him, along with his pack of wolves who aren't perverts, so you might as well start looking elsewhere for another conduit because you're not getting that one."

The two wolves looked to Trevor. "Is that true?" asked the bigger of the two males.

Trevor winced, as though there was a threat somewhere in the question.

Maybe there was.

"I think so. I couldn't get that close, but that's pretty much what I heard, too. I think."

Trevor glared at her, as though daring her to contradict him.

Taylor blinked at Trevor, wondering why he didn't tell the wolves where the three men had gone. He'd come back home fairly quickly; maybe he couldn't bring himself to follow after the three shifters when he had to rush back here and rat out her and Jonas.

What an asshole.

Then she got an idea. "Look, you guys, I don't want anything bad to happen to my baby. If you want to know anything, ask, and Jonas and I will tell you everything Trevor kept from you."

Trevor damn near jumped three feet in the air. "What?"

The two wolves looked at Trevor, and he backed up a step, his hands up as though getting ready to ward off an attack. "She-she's lying! I didn't keep anything from you! I swear!"

Part of her felt sorry for this, but another part of her felt alive and powerful. She felt like a warrior ready to lay down her life and safety for her little girl, and she was willing to make this gamble.

Jonas watched on. Either because he had no choice, or he was putting his trust in her that she knew what to do as one of the wolves stepped up to her, ignoring the knife in her hand while his larger counterpart continued to get closer and closer to Trevor.

"This had better be good. What did he hide from us?"

Taylor swallowed. "All right, well, Trevor was there when Steve, the man mated to the conduit you wanted, told us his mate is pregnant with their first child."

Which was something she was totally making up at that moment, but it didn't matter so long as it put all the attention on Trevor, and none of it onto her or Jonas.

"That's a lie! I didn't hear that at all!"

"Trevor, I could see you standing right there. You weren't doing that good of a job hiding. There's no way you didn't hear that."

It had to be the worst lie in the history of lies. Maybe that was why the wolves seemed to believe it. It was such a stupid thing for someone to make up, and too dangerous to risk. That was the explanation Taylor was going to go with as the two wolf shifters turned their backs onto Jonas and Taylor as they suddenly started stalking towards Trevor.

The low growls they let out, along with the way every hair on their tails seemed to stand on end, made it the meanest looking sight Taylor had ever seen, and she was a little sorry to have sicced the wolves after Trevor like that.

Whatever. He would live.

Maybe.

Jonas gestured for the door.

Taylor nodded. Even if they'd face more wolves and bears when they left her trailer, at least they'd be closer to freedom and getting Meg to safety. Hell, she was already planning on shoving Meg into Jonas' arms and having him make a run for it so she could shift into her bear form and give him as much time as he needed to get out of there with their daughter.

They bolted for the door, Jonas skidding in behind her before she could go along with her plans of noble sacrifice.

"Run!" The wolves turned their attention back to them as they realized she and Jonas were making a break for it.

Taylor ran. She wanted to stay, even scared as she was; she didn't want to leave him alone to fight, but she had Meg. It always boiled down to protecting her daughter. So she ran.

Her bear ears picked up the sound of a wolf's high-pitched cry behind her. One of them must have run into the knife Jonas still had. She could see members of her sloth around her as she moved with her child. No one interfered. They watched her go, some looking very much as though they wanted to go with her.

Maybe they didn't think she would get away. Maybe that was why they didn't try stopping her.

She took the road, avoiding the woods for now. If she got lucky, someone might come driving up here. Preferably a non-local who was a little lost. It happened sometimes. She could get a ride.

But if the wolves came for her, she would turn to the woods then.

But she didn't hear anyone coming up behind her. Just the sound of her heavy breathing as she kept her pace steady, and Meg's cries in protest of all the jostling. "It's okay. We're all right." Taylor wasn't sure whose benefit she said it for. "We're okay."

She had to keep going. If she strained her ears hard enough, she could make out the sound of the wolves fighting. She didn't want to think about what they were doing to Jonas, or what he was putting himself through to keep them away from her, to give her enough time.

Five more minutes. Maybe ten. She just had to keep running. She was so close to the main road. There would be more lights there and a better chance of getting a truck to stop for her.

Almost there. Almost.

A bear roared in the background. A noise so terrible and ongoing it made Taylor stop and look back.

Was that...no, it couldn't be. He wouldn't...

Taylor kept going, running away from the danger and horror that was taking place in her sloth's territory.

One foot in front of the other. She repeated it again and again, even when she saw headlights coming up behind her.

She ducked into the trees so she could get a look at the

vehicle's driver before asking for help. She was at the part of the woods that had already been burned. The smell of soot here was strong, and she wouldn't have much cover against other shifters who already had next to perfect night vision.

"Taylor! Wait!"

Jonas' voice was the only thing that could have stopped her. She nearly tripped over a burned tree root when spinning around. She could see him, getting out of the truck and limply pulling himself around to the front. He wasn't driving. Someone else was.

Andrew.

"Come on! We have to go."

He waved her over. Even with the way he cradled his arm, he still stood strong. Proud.

Alive.

She ran to him, only just then realizing how badly her side hurt as she gasped for breath, crying.

Jonas opened his good arm, wrapping her and Meg up in it. She felt his lips in her hair and the relief in his voice.

"Let's go."

"You smell like blood."

"I'm fine." He pulled her to the passenger side of the truck, and she realized a lot of the blood was coming from his leg. "Come on."

She didn't fight him on it. Taylor went, pulling herself into the passenger side of the truck and holding Meg on her lap. It put her up close and personal with Andrew, who sat immediately next to her in the driver's seat.

"Hey, kiddo."

Taylor said nothing, and then Jonas groaned as he

pulled himself next to Taylor, squishing her between both men.

"Let's get out of here," Jonas rasped, letting his head fall back onto the seat as his good hand rested lightly on Meg's arm.

"You got it." Andrew started to drive, and Taylor had to wonder what planet she was on.

CHAPTER 19

" *L* et me see your arm."

Taylor wasn't ready to look at Andrew to ask what the hell he'd been up to, or why he was bothering with helping them.

"It's fine." It wasn't fine. She could see it in the way his jaw clenched.

"Jonas, please let me see."

He looked at her. She stared back at him. Jonas sighed, leaning a little closer.

The blood wasn't gushing, which was a good sign, but there was still a lot of it, and it was still dark and red and...God, she could smell it. Her inner black bear growled, not at all impressed with the way her mate had been attacked.

She tucked Meg safely in Jonas' good arm, and then pulled some of the torn material of Jonas' jacket and shirt out of the way to get a better look at the wound.

It was a bite wound. He would live, but something had gotten him. She was no doctor, and it wasn't exactly well lit in the truck cab, so she couldn't tell what sort of bite it was. Jonas had the smell of wolves and bears on him, so that didn't help.

"Who was it?" Taylor tried to keep the growl out of her voice and decided to keep from looking back at Andrew. She didn't want to admit that she blamed him for this, but it was there.

"A wolf, but I got him back good, don't worry." He smiled through his pain, but it looked to be genuine. Taylor wasn't so sure how much she trusted that smile, but she would roll with it for now. As long as he didn't look to be in any danger, she would be happy with what he presented her with.

"Found out what the wolves want," Andrew growled.

Taylor looked back at him, trying not to glare, and failing because Jonas' blood was on her free hand, and now she was stuck trying not to touch Meg with it.

"We know what they want. They want a conduit."

Andrew shook his head. "Not just a conduit. They wanted to get someone back. Revenge for someone who wronged a family member. Tale as old as time."

"Revenge?" Taylor didn't know if she believed that. Not after everything she already knew. "We didn't hurt anyone, though. Did we?"

Andrew seemed to take offense to the suspicion in her voice. "Of course we didn't!"

"I thought this was about helping them find the conduit they wanted?" Jonas suddenly hissed, and Taylor yanked her hand back from his arm, only then realizing she was clenching it too damned tight. "I'm sorry!"

Meg fussed again. In a minute or two, she would be full blown crying.

"They did come to me for that, but that wasn't the whole goddamned story," Andrew said. He clenched the steering wheel so hard Taylor worried he might bend it out of shape.

"What did they tell you?" Taylor asked. "Tell me the truth; if you lie to me after the danger you put Meg into—"

"Hey! Don't give me that shit. All right? I kept her safe when those wolves came back here to sniff around. I didn't let a damned thing happen to that little girl, and I never would have. You understand me?"

Taylor growled, but what could she say to that? She still wasn't so sure if she trusted Andrew, but right about now, if her mother had still been around, she might not trust her either.

The person who mattered the most right now was squirming in Jonas' arms. Anyone or anything that behaved suspiciously got little to no benefit of the doubt as far as Taylor was concerned.

"Tell us the whole story, Andrew." Jonas sounded just as pissed off as Taylor felt. "Right now. No bullshit. I want to know what the hell is going on with those stupid wolves. Good people are injured, and some of them are dead."

Taylor winced, remembering those injured in the firehouse. One of whom was a good friend and colleague of Jonas'.

"Apparently, the pack that has the conduit caught a wolf sniffing around her, wanting to make a claim."

Taylor didn't understand where this was going. "And?"

"The conduit's mate didn't like this. He and some buddies caught and tortured the kid for getting too close. Damn near killed him before finally letting him go."

"Kid?" Jonas asked, lifting a brow.

"Not an actual kid, some idiot early twenties type." Taylor had never heard the growl that came from Andrew's voice. It was strange. And it was scary.

"I don't doubt for one minute the wolves played up the story, making their little prick of a friend look more innocent than he actually was, but that's not the point. That kid was the younger brother of his pack's alpha. He goes home covered in blood and crying, and then his big brother wants revenge. They want the conduit, and revenge on the wolf pack that tortured one of their own."

"But they needed to secure alliances before the war started," Taylor surmised.

Andrew nodded. "When we refused to help the first time, the fires started. Now they've set up shop on my fucking territory, and I'm stuck dealing with their shit while trying to keep everyone safe." Andrew looked at her, his eyes narrowed. "You're welcome, by the way."

Taylor's spine stiffened. A sudden wave of shame hit her hard. She had to look away from him just because she didn't like that she'd accused him of something so terrible, that she'd believed he...what? That he might have invited the wolves over? That he might have been involved with the fires this entire time?

Light appeared behind them in the distance. It was a strange thing, to look back and to wonder who was there when Taylor never had to worry about such a thing before in her entire life.

Jonas put his good hand on her shoulder and tried to

push her down. At least, that's what Taylor thought he was doing. She couldn't be sure because she was so focused on watching the oncoming headlights that she didn't go down. When the vehicle eventually passed them by, and Taylor was able to see for herself that it was a couple of college-aged girls in the front seat, she relaxed, heaving a sigh when she barely realized she was holding her breath.

"I need to get off this road," Andrew growled. His claws were coming out as he gripped the steering wheel so tight he looked like he was going to bend the wheel. "If they're not getting ready to drive up from behind then they might be trying to chase us down."

"Bring us back to the police station," Jonas said. "We can get everything we need dealt with right there."

Andrew growled a little. Taylor expected a fight for involving the humans, but he nodded. "Yeah, got it."

"You mean you'll take us?" Taylor couldn't believe it. She looked down at Meg, who had stopped fussing, likely due to the comforting rumble of the truck engine.

Things were starting to look up.

Before Andrew could answer, glass shattered inward on the driver's side window.

Everything moved in slow motion. Taylor felt the spray of glass and heat against her face. She turned towards Jonas, trying to protect Meg from the flying shards. Jonas wrapped his arm around her shoulders and pulled her to him. But even without looking back, she felt the teeth snapping behind her, and then Jonas' arms almost didn't seem strong enough to hold onto her as Andrew slammed his foot onto the brake.

The truck screeched and fishtailed. She thought she

was going to go flying out the windshield. The momentum pushed her against Jonas instead.

He grabbed onto her, holding tight. She wanted to tell him to hold onto Meg, to keep their baby from being thrown from the vehicle and to not bother with her. But just as fast as the truck was attacked and Andrew slammed on the brakes, it all stopped.

Meg cried, long and loud wails from being disturbed and then being squeezed. Taylor didn't care. She pulled her baby into her arms. Jonas gripped her shoulder with his good arm, tight enough that it should have hurt, but she barely felt it. "Are you all right? Look at me! Are you okay?"

Taylor nodded, looking down at Meg, who was wailing miserably, tears streaming down her chubby cheeks and her soft little bear ears. All Taylor could think about was how happy she was, how utterly grateful she felt, to have her daughter still in her arms. She held Meg a little tighter, even knowing her little girl didn't like it. Taylor kissed her face, her cheeks, and her hair.

Taylor's entire body trembled. She'd been so focused on trying to get away that she didn't think about the lack of a car seat, or how she wasn't buckled in.

Neither was Jonas. Taylor only realized that when his trembling hand released the seatbelt. He must have grabbed onto it, then reached for Taylor the instant Andrew slammed his foot onto the brake.

Which meant he'd held her as tightly as he had with his wounded arm.

His body trembled, and there was so little color in his cheeks considering what had just happened, but he didn't look to be in any pain. No. Jonas seemed as alert and ready as though he was planning on rushing to the nearest house fire so he could put it out.

"You sure you're good?"

The ringing in Taylor's ears eventually came to a stop, and before she could answer, it hit her that there was still someone else in the truck.

"Andrew."

She glanced back at her alpha. Jonas said her name, but he suddenly sounded so very far away as she looked at the bloody mess that was her leader and friend.

Now she knew why she felt teeth behind her.

With all the blood on his face, the entire left side of his body mangled, she didn't think he would be able to tell her how he felt for a long time.

If ever.

She snapped out of it. "Jesus Christ, Andrew!"

"Don't!"

Jonas grabbed her by the arm, yanking her back before she could grab him, shake him, make sure he was alive.

Please, be alive.

She couldn't hear a heartbeat, but there was still a heavy rumbling all around her and the sounds of Meg's crying.

"Taylor, don't touch him, his foot is still on the brake."

"What?"

Jonas pointed down, and that was when she saw it.

Whether Andrew was dead or not, he was still keeping the truck stopped.

Jonas reached forward, put the truck into park, and then turned the engine. "We have to go."

Taylor reached out, pressing her fingers to the side of his neck. She still couldn't hear a heartbeat, but that could be because Meg wanted to get out of there and was making that need known as loud as she possibly could.

Jonas pulled on her arm. "Taylor! We need to go!"

She didn't want to leave Andrew to die here, if he was even still alive.

"Taylor!"

It wasn't just Jonas screaming for her. Meg's shrieks reminded her that they weren't out of danger yet, and there was no time to spare if they wanted to get away.

Not even for a friend. For someone who was basically her family.

Taylor let herself be pulled outside by Jonas, and she didn't look back at the friend she was leaving behind.

CHAPTER 20

Jonas knew what he was asking, pulling Taylor away from Andrew. He was more than just a friend to her; he was someone who had taken care of her when she had no one else. He hated to leave Andrew behind, but he'd seen the snapping teeth of the wolf who busted his snout in through the driver's side window, and he didn't want teeth like that coming anywhere near Taylor or his little girl.

His arm started to burn and throb again now that the adrenaline rush of the crash was done and over with.

Fuck. He held onto his arm, trying to hold back the building pressure, but it was difficult.

"Can you smell anything around here? Are they still around?" His sense of smell was ineffective because of all the blood. Taylor's full shifter senses would still be sharp though.

She took in several breaths, holding control of herself despite Meg's hollering in her arms. He wanted to take the little girl to give her mother a chance to focus, but he didn't trust that he would be able to hold her properly with only one arm.

Taylor glanced back at the truck, and then down the road. He could see what she looked at, and he was pretty sure he had a good idea of what it was, but he went to take a closer look anyway.

"Don't." Taylor's eyes were wide. She shook her head. "Don't look."

"Is it dead?"

"I think so, but just...stay away from it. Please."

He wanted to stay back, but he couldn't. Something inside of him compelled to go over there and make sure for himself that it wasn't about to chase after them.

As he approached, he saw the wolf was a big one. It seemed lifeless; the chest didn't rise and fall with any breathing. There wasn't even any sign that the damned thing had been running at all. Even the best of shifters panted for breath when they'd been running like that.

And this was one deathly still.

Jonas could see why when he stood right next to it.

Its tail and hind leg were both mangled. When it crashed into the truck and tried to kill them, it must have gotten caught in the back tire and pulled under, crunching its middle.

That was gross.

Jonas sneered down at the body.

Too bad Andrew couldn't have turned this fleabag into roadkill before it slashed his throat open.

"Jonas, we need to go, please. I can hear others coming."

He nodded. The pain in his arm flared up again. This

one must have been faster than the rest, but it didn't matter now because he had to get his mate and child out of here. To safety.

He turned and ran back to where Taylor stood. She reached her hand out. He took it, stunned with the strength she gripped his hand with. "Thank you."

"For what?"

Taylor didn't say. When she pulled him into the woods, he let her lead the way. She was the one with a bear shifter's sense of smell. She would know the best direction to go.

God, Jonas wished he had his ax right about now.

"Can we make it into town?"

Taylor didn't say. Meg wouldn't stop wailing. He wanted to quiet her, but he didn't know a thing about how to keep babies silent. He didn't blame the little girl for being upset after all that had happened, but at the same time, silence would give them a better chance of getting away. She was a siren call to anyone and anything that wanted to hunt them down.

"Taylor, can we make it into town?" Her lack of an answer didn't bode well with him.

He intended on getting her to answer him, except she suddenly stopped, thrust Meg into his arms before he could say a word about it, and backed off.

"What are you doing?" He focused on holding the little girl with his good arm, using his bad one to keep her balance. "Taylor, come on, we've got to move."

"You're not going to get away with Meg like this. I'll hold them off."

His gut clenched. When she shifted into her black bear form, he wanted to yell at her for even thinking it would be a good idea to do something like that without his say.

"Taylor! Don't even think about it! Come on! Right now!"

She needed to listen to him. He needed to get her over here. To get her back before she did something they were both going to regret the hell out of.

He couldn't lose her.

"Taylor!"

She didn't listen. The bear regarded him and Meg, snorted, then turned and faced the sounds of the howls floating up in the distance.

The wolves were almost here.

Meg shrieked louder, as though she knew something was amiss. Her chubby arms reached out as the bear began to charge, but Taylor stopped short when a red fox jumped into her path.

Jonas didn't wait for something else to happen. He rushed forward. Meg still screamed in his arms, but he couldn't stop. He had to get to the black bear before she ran off. Jonas put his hand onto her fur when he made it to her, ignoring the heat and throb in his arm.

"Don't leave. Your daughter needs you."

Taylor seemed to be having a staring contest with the fox. He looked at it when Taylor refused to pay him atten- tion. The fox was dark in color. The only bit of orange seemed to be in a puff on its chest.

He narrowed his eyes at those ears. Wasn't that…

The fox shifted, revealing a slender woman, beautiful —although to him she didn't have anything on Taylor— with dark brunette hair and matching dark fox ears on her head, her dark tail waiving around behind her.

How she managed to move around in jeans that tight was beyond him, but he recognized this woman. This was the woman from the station where he'd found the injured and dead men.

Jonas' first instinct was to step in front of Taylor. He had to stop himself when he realized he was still holding onto his screaming daughter. "What do you want?"

"We have to get out of here." She reached into the pocket of her leather jacket, producing a phone. She showed it to him, and to Taylor. "You met up with my brother and a few friends earlier, right?"

She showed off the picture. He saw Link there, and Steve.

"You're Zelda?"

"That's me."

He still wasn't sure this meant he should trust her, and Jonas found himself holding onto Meg a little tighter despite her screaming. "So what do you want?"

"For you to come with me." She pocketed the phone. "You saved my mate's life. Those people are chasing you. I can smell them coming."

Taylor snorted, as though she agreed with the statement.

Another howl, sounding slower than the previous one, confirmed this.

"Tell me that brother and friends of yours are around here?" Jonas wouldn't mind having the backup right about now.

Zelda shook her head. "They don't know I'm here. Link would kill me. My uncle would help him. I came because it was stupid for them to leave you alone. I just wanted to get close and make sure everything was all right. It's not, so come on."

She started to move, running through the woods in a completely different direction from the road and the sounds of the howls. Jonas looked at Taylor. The bear stared back at him as though she didn't want to trust a woman who just appeared out of nowhere.

Jonas got that, but they didn't have time to think this over. "We have to. For Meg." He chased after the fox woman without glancing back, hoping that Taylor would follow. He smiled when he heard the snorting and snuffling of the bear chasing after him; then he spotted it in his peripheral vision.

He didn't look at Taylor. If he smiled at her right now, it might rub her the wrong way that they were changing course. Even though he wished she would get back into her human shape, he was glad for this.

She wanted to fight the wolves and protect her daughter. This mama bear was going to have to cool it on that one because Jonas did not want her doing that. Taylor could stay in her bear shape all she wanted, waiting for something to attack them, but so long as it didn't come down to that, Jonas was all right.

He had to start paying attention to where he was putting his feet. He might be subhuman, but it was getting to the point where it was too dark for even him to see properly.

And Taylor growled at him every time he caught himself tripping. Meg didn't appreciate that either. Still, he managed to keep up. "Where are you taking us?"

"To my car."

Car? There were no roads out here. Unless one had been built when he was away?

Eventually, with the howls behind them getting closer and closer, they made it to what was definitely not a road. It was more of a path. Probably something the odd hiker and animal used. The car sat there, parked, taking up almost all the space there was for it.

It was as though the trees were trying to hug the damned thing. Or swallow it up.

"You've got to be shitting me."

Another howl.

Close. So close he worried one of the bastards would get the jump on him.

Taylor growled, a dangerous noise, as she looked behind her. She might even be able to see their shadows closing in.

Jonas went to the passenger side of the car. It was difficult to open the door without the branches of the trees immediately trying to get in, but he kept his eye on Taylor as Zelda managed to pull herself into the driver's side of the vehicle.

When she started the engine and Taylor still was not inside of the car, Jonas began to to worry.

"Taylor! Come on!"

If this fox girl tried to drive away without her…

Then Jonas would put Meg into the car and let the both of them go because he wasn't about to run away when his mate needed backup.

Zelda didn't seem to enjoy the wait any more than Jonas did. She yelled out of the driver's side window. "Hurry up!"

Taylor glanced back, as though finally realizing that time was of the essence. She shifted so fast that Jonas could have blinked and missed it. Her eyes stayed a bright shade of gold, however. The animal was still very much there, just beneath the surface and ready to fight if need be.

Finally. She pulled open the door to the back passenger seat and got in. Jonas did at the same time. His ass was barely in place when Zelda hit the gas.

Not one second too soon either. He'd just managed to get the door shut and locked, and was looking back at Taylor, debating if he should kiss her or yell at her, when he caught sight of the wolves running onto them.

"Drive faster," he commanded.

Taylor looked back, too. Jonas heard her growling.

Zelda floored it. He felt the tires spin, and the vehicle fishtail a bit while dust and rocks spit up all around them. The dirt road with all of its bumps and dips prevented her from going as fast as Jonas would have liked, but they kept ahead of the wolves. It was only seconds, but it seemed forever, before the pack grew smaller and smaller behind them, until they were out of view and far enough gone that Jonas could breathe again.

Taylor looked at him. The gold was still in her eyes, but there was something more vulnerable there too. She didn't seem ready for a fight anymore. She looked as though she couldn't believe they'd just escaped.

Then she took note of her child.

"Baby, come here."

Taylor held her hands out. Jonas didn't hesitate to help Meg into her arms. The crying quieted slightly. It only made sense that Meg would be more comfortable in the arms of her mother. She still didn't know Jonas.

The ache he would have felt over coming to terms with that wasn't there. Jonas was more concerned with the woman behind the wheel.

"Tell me what your pack or skulk or whatever has to do with those wolves setting these fires. Right now."

Zelda clenched her hands around the wheel. "All right."

CHAPTER 21

The road didn't get any less dark or bumpy as Zelda started talking. Jonas was still acutely aware of everything around him. Every moving shadow, every scratch on the side of the car from the reaching tree branches. If one of those wolves appeared and tried busting through the windows again, he was going to be ready.

"So because your ex-husband killed your alpha you ran away and then found your natural mate, who happens to be a bodyguard. Then your mate's best friend was attacked by shifters, changed into a wolf shifter, and found his mate who turned out to be a conduit being stalked by a whole other pack of wolves who may or may not be connected to your old pack. This guy, Steve, helped torture one of their members for attempting to rape his mate…Jesus Christ, am I getting this right so far?" Jonas looked back at Taylor to make sure he wasn't hearing things, and when she gave him a similar look of disbelief, he almost didn't believe it.

Zelda's neck tightened. She nodded. "That's basically it. Yeah. Yeah…"

She sounded embarrassed. Jonas wasn't sure why she didn't seem worried. She had every reason to be worried right about now, considering the wolf shifters who were out there wanted to tear into him and Taylor.

He didn't even want to think about the fact that he'd left Andrew behind…

Taylor leaned forward.

"I didn't know any of this. I thought those wolves just wanted us to help them get the conduit they wanted. I never heard anything about a little brother being tortured."

Taylor looked at Jonas. "I swear I never knew that."

Jonas nodded. "I believe you."

Taylor had managed to get Meg to quiet down a little. She hiccupped a little, her chubby little face still wet with tears, and she was gripping her mother's tear-stained shirt with tiny, fiercely-clenched hands.

Jonas nearly reached out to touch her, but he doubted the little girl would want anyone other than her mother after what happened.

So he kept his hands to himself.

"I believe you. You and Andrew are close, but I don't think he would have been comfortable with telling you everything that was going on."

Especially as the alpha of the clan. Every alpha kept a few things to himself. That was just the way things worked with them. They wanted what was best for their packs and clans; they made deals, they kept secrets.

This was apparently one of them.

The wolf pack had come asking for help in retrieving a

conduit they wanted, but they also wanted revenge on that same conduit and her mate for the torture of the alpha's little brother.

Jonas didn't need to have siblings to know the lengths some siblings would go to, to defend each other. Or get their revenge.

"The fires weren't all about Andrew's refusal to help. They were trying to lure you and your friends out of hiding, weren't they?"

"Something like that," Zelda said. "My skulk isn't far from here either. Neither is Jackson's pack. This was supposed to be a warning to everyone. They'll burn it all down, even their own land to show us how serious they are. They just want us to burn with them at this point."

"Jesus," Taylor breathed.

Jonas hated this more and more. Why couldn't this shit be simple? Why was nothing ever easy?

Bad guys wanted to get their hands on a conduit. Perfect. He could wrap his mind around that one, no problem.

Bad guys wanted to get their hands on a conduit, and get revenge for a tortured relative, sure… but going on to destroy acres of their own land?

"Wait, this means they're nearby. This is a local pack."

Zelda nodded. "Yeah."

"So, where are we going?" Taylor asked.

"Somewhere safe." The conviction in her voice was so firm Jonas almost trusted her. He was still wary, but with the werewolves chasing after him, and Taylor half ready to go charging into action, he wasn't so sure if he had much of a choice.

He wasn't about to let Taylor rush off and get killed, leaving him and Meg behind. Forget that.

Taylor barely seemed capable of holding back her inner bear even now. She pushed Meg back into Jonas' arms, which was something the little girl clearly wanted no part of, if the way she started crying again was any indicator. He felt weird holding her away from her mother, but the black fur starting to come in through Taylor's pores gave him the feeling that she was getting ready for a fast transformation in case it turned out they couldn't trust Zelda after all.

Or she just couldn't hold it back with the stress she was under.

Jonas looked at Zelda. She kept her eyes on the road, but he knew she was aware of the way he looked at her. "If this turns out to be some kind of trap or trick, it won't matter that I'm a subhuman. I will find a way to make you and everyone you love pay for it."

She didn't cower at the threat. He wasn't sure whether or not that was a good sign. Instead, Zelda nodded. "Understood."

They drove into the night, though it wasn't lost on Jonas the way Zelda's fox ears and Taylor's bear ears both twitched when another long, watery howl sounded off behind them.

CHAPTER 22

When Zelda told them she was taking them someplace safe, Taylor didn't think the woman would actually take them to the local motel where Taylor worked before she opened up her daycare.

She came to a stop in front of one of the doors marked one-one-nine.

"You've got to be kidding me."

"Nope." Zelda killed the engine and exited the vehicle, taking the keys with her before anyone could ask more questions.

Jonas looked at her. "You can take Meg, and I'll go check it out."

She bristled at that. "And what do you think you're going to do if a group of shifters are in there waiting for you?"

"I can hold off a few people, give you and Meg the chance to get out of here. Or we can steal the car and get out of here together. I don't mind either way, just so you know."

The selfish part of her wanted to take that offer, but one look into Meg's unhappy face was enough to push her out of the car and towards the motel room, despite Jonas' protests.

She felt him fall into step beside her. "If anyone tries anything, Jonas, you're the one who's going to take Meg and run for it. Understand me?" She already had her claws ready.

He glared at her but said nothing.

She had no idea how Zelda or her friends had managed to stay here without the wolf shifters knowing about it, but that could mean there wasn't a lot of time to stick around here. If that were the case, Taylor would pry those car keys from Zelda's fingers herself and make sure Jonas had them.

If he could drive, then his chances for escape would be better.

Taylor just wished she could get her hands on a car seat so Meg would have something safer to ride in, but beggars couldn't be choosers.

She pounded on the door.

It opened for her before her fist finished slamming on the wood.

Jackson stood there. He didn't look remotely impressed to see her, but considering what she'd just gone through, the feeling was mutual.

Taylor inflated her courage, ignoring the reminder that she'd met this man only once, and that was on the side of the road after getting caught making love to her mate. She knew nothing about him that made her believe he was an ally. "Hi. I hear it's safer to be here right now."

Her nose picked up scents that indicated several people waited inside.

He nodded. "It might be."

Taylor was not about to let her daughter into that room before she had a few things out of the way. "How do we know you're not working with the wolves? That this isn't some trap?"

The man looked at her. The wolf ears on top of his bald head twitching. He raised a brow at her before looking back at Jonas.

"It's a fair question, we don't know you people," Jonas said, sounding irritable. He didn't enter the room, which was good since he was still the one holding onto Meg.

Taylor was so damned happy he had her back on this. She didn't know what she would have done if he didn't.

"We all want the same thing. A stop to the wolves," Jackson said. "By any means necessary."

Taylor blinked at that. "That sounds real safe. Like the motto of a hoard of outlaws." She couldn't hide how much she distrusted this whole thing, so why bother with trying?

"I can assure you; you are safe here," Jackson said. "The wolves want our heads, too."

"Aren't you a wolf?" Taylor looked at his ears.

Jackson grinned at her. "If these wolves were in my pack, they wouldn't even think about doing half the things they were doing now. They would know there would be consequences. Not all packs have that."

She couldn't shake the weird feeling she had about this guy. Taylor didn't want to be anywhere near him. "Right, Jonas, I still say we can steal the car and get out of here without them."

Jonas inhaled a deep breath, closed his eyes, then looked at her. "Might not be the best thing to say in front of them, sweetheart."

He hadn't smiled at her and called her sweetheart like that in a long time. Strange how she was noticing the little things right when this was entirely not the time.

She smiled right back at him. "I don't care what these people think of me, sweetheart," she said back, batting her eyes before looking right at Jackson. "If they fuck around with Meg or me or you, then I'll take everything they've got and leave them for dead."

After what happened to Andrew, she wasn't about to take the risk that anything else would go wrong.

Jackson smiled. "I like your woman."

"Yeah, great, keep your eyes to yourself, pal."

The people inside the room apparently got sick of the exchange, because a male voice called out to them. "Jackson, will you stop that."

"Let them in already," Zelda's voice snapped. "They're leaving their scent all over out there."

Which was true.

Jackson opened the door wider, revealing his friends inside. Zelda was there, along with the two other men Taylor had met before with Jackson; Link and Steve.

They stared at her with a strange hesitation. As though they didn't know what to do with Taylor or Jonas now that they were here.

Taylor hesitated. Jonas seemed to be waiting for her to make the decision. It was Zelda who was able to get her to come in.

"Come on, before your scent gets out too much." She waved them over.

Maybe it was because it was another woman saying it, but Taylor found the power to step over the threshold. Once inside, Jonas followed her with Meg.

When Jackson closed the door, her inner wild animal puffed itself up.

"Just so you all know, if any of you try anything to hurt that little girl, I can turn into a bear, a big one, and it can do a lot of damage before any of you get anywhere near here. Understand?"

Zelda shook her head, her eyes wide, as though she was hurt Taylor would suggest such a thing. "No one here is going to hurt your baby."

"And you wouldn't be able to carry through with the threat even if we were intimidating her," Jackson said.

Taylor decided she didn't like him. She glared at the other man as he stepped into the center of the room. The others in the room looked at him with equal parts shock and disgust.

Steve stepped forward. His trimmed auburn hair and three-day old shave let Taylor know it had been a while since he'd rested. He looked like he might have been in a scuffle or even a full-blown fight. "Please ignore my idiot friend here. He doesn't human too well."

"No kidding, can you at least tell him he can take his attitude and shove it where..." She trailed off, suddenly aware of something that had been unknown to her before.

Steve was a shifter. He didn't have the ears or the tail, but she felt it in the air. It was so evident by smell, now that he stood so close to her in this confined space.

"You're a wolf." She stepped away. Taylor kept looking up at his head, waiting for something to appear to show her what she already knew. "How?" "I was turned. No ears and tail for me." Steve scratched at his hair, smiling bashfully, and she wondered if it were something he wished he could have. "Couldn't you tell the last time we met?"

She ignored the question. "Turned. And you're the one who tortured the wolf's brother?"

The smile immediately slipped from Steve's face.

Taylor looked at Zelda. "You said your mate's friend's name was Steve, right? The guy who was involved in what happened?"

"I said that."

Zelda looked a little unsure about admitting to that now. In fact, she looked as though she didn't want to be here, period.

Taylor looked back at Steve, then backed up towards Jonas. She was finally starting to piece together everything she'd learned from Andrew, and Zelda, and Steve himself. Starting to understand the depth of trouble that these shifters had brought to her sloth. "Forget this. Let's get out of here."

"Baby—"

"No, this is the guy who brought all this down on us. You tortured some kid? Are you serious? Why am I even in the same room as you?"

Steve narrowed his eyes. "What do you mean kid? What did you tell her?" He looked at Zelda, who shrugged her shoulders helplessly.

"She told us everything. That the wolves are here for your mate, and that the two of you tortured some kid who went after her, and now his big brother is punishing my sloth, went after my alpha because you couldn't control your fucking temper!"

Taylor could barely control her temper either. Otherwise, she never would have sworn like that when her daughter was within hearing distance.

"I didn't say he tortured a kid. Just because he was a younger brother to the alpha doesn't mean he had some youth of innocence to hide behind."

"I don't care."

Ever since Taylor had Meg, anyone under the age of twenty had seemed like a kid to her. Which she knew was a strange way to think of it considering her own age.

Jonas stepped next to her. "Taylor, we need these people."

"No, we don't. How do we know where they draw the line if they're willing to torture?" She didn't look at her daughter. Taylor had her sights on the bastard in front of her, and she wasn't about to look away in case any back-stabbing occurred.

"Uh, should we maybe rethink having these people around here?" Link asked. He didn't give off an alpha vibe, which was probably why she'd been able to ignore that he was there until now.

"No," Zelda said. "The wolves are after them now, too. Personally. They've got a baby. We can't just throw them out after we got them involved."

"I wish I knew what the hell you were even doing out there," Link said, glaring at Zelda. Taylor could see the similarities in features between the siblings and under-stood Link's concern for her, but Taylor's only interest was in Meg. Everyone else could rot in hell for all she cared.

"I was helping the people who are in danger through no fault of their own!"

Everyone was talking over each other. Arguing over

whether or not to keep Jonas and Taylor here, what they could or couldn't do, and all the voices were starting to irritate the bear inside Taylor's head. She felt its growling, the way it stomped its massive paws inside her skull, wanting out, wanting to fight and defend.

Wanting revenge for Andrew.

She didn't know how much longer she could hold back. She hadn't had trouble holding the animal back like this since the first time she'd turned, and with so many people in the same room, no one trusting each other, she knew she couldn't just let it out.

But the bear wanted out. So badly.

"All right, everyone stop," Jonas snapped.

Taylor's eyes flew open. She hadn't even been aware of closing them. Jonas glared at each and everyone in the room, shocking Taylor with the way he'd managed to get command of the situation.

She was also shocked by the way he looked at her while he held onto their daughter. "Christ, Taylor, I know you want to protect Meg, but we are not going out there without any backup. End of story. I can see all of your ears twitching. I know you can hear the wolves. They're looking for us right now."

Taylor clenched her hands to fists. She looked at Jonas, at her mate. Strangely, with the way he stood and the way he spoke, the animal inside of her brain acted as though he was the alpha in the room.

And it was hot. As hot as it was annoying, given their present situation. "We don't need them. It might be just as dangerous to be here as it is to go it on our own."

"We can't." The dead look in Jonas' eyes was what got her. "We can't do this on our own. Andrew is gone. You can't go back home with Trevor there, or the wolves." He leaned closer, his voice a cool, smooth balm on her wounded pride, and her pained soul. "You have to put aside the nature of the sloth to hate the other packs, and you have to let us all work together now. It's just you, me, and Meg, and I need you with me on this."

Her heart ached to hear that. She'd wanted to hear words like that for the longest time.

She'd just never wanted to hear them under these conditions.

Taylor sucked back a breath. She felt the itch of her fur sliding back under her pores. Her daughter was quiet now. Meg had cried herself to sleep, and now it seemed as though there was no going back.

This was where they were. This was the situation she had to deal with.

Because the wolves were out there, howling at each other and searching for her and her daughter.

A murderous bunch. That was what Steve had called them.

Before he'd decided to be a complete asshole and hide information from her.

She would not let those wolves near her child.

Taylor inhaled a deep breath. "Will you please help me to keep Meg safe? I can't go home with the wolves there."

Or with Trevor fucking everything up for her.

Link and Zelda both smiled, as though they were grateful for the change in attitude.

Steve's smile was much more subdued. He held out his hand to her. "We'll do whatever we can to get you through this."

Taylor looked at it, then at Jackson, whose expression remained neutral and unreadable.

Jonas' face was just as stoic, but she could see it in his eyes that this was what he wanted.

She took Steve's hand, shaking it. "Thank you."

The bang on the front door made her, and everyone else in the room jump.

They all turned to the door. Steve pulled a gun from a holster hidden behind his back. Jackson growled and revealed his teeth.

Another bang against the door made it bend inwards a little, and then the howling started.

CHAPTER 23

Jonas backed up from the door, his skin crawling when he heard the long scratches down the other side of the door.

The fact that Steve was going to use a gun when he was shifter was comforting.

"I need a weapon," he said, glancing around for anything he could use with one arm holding onto a baby and the other still out of commission.

Meg had woken up at the sound of the banging, but she didn't cry. She rested her head against his chest and whimpered slightly, but seemed to have no strength left to protest.

Holding her, however, was just a reminder of how fragile this little girl was. He didn't want anything coming near her. He wasn't going to let anything go near her.

"Taylor, you need to take Meg. Let us hold them off, and get out of her, find a ride with someone driving by."

Taylor shook her head, the blue in her hair glinting under the lamplight. Fur grew in from the pores on her arms. Her eyes were a bright shade of gold. "No, you hold onto her. I'm going to face this now, not be on the run from them forever."

Even as she said it, Jonas went to the phone and dialed nine-one-one. He left it off the hook to ring, and took Meg back to the bathroom, the safest distance away from the banging.

Police and other first responders would trace the call and come out if they had the right tracers. He just hoped they heard enough of what was going on to know to send a lot of people.

"They've stopped slamming on the door," Jackson said.

That was what Jonas noticed it, too. There was no more banging, which was strange because one more hard slam and that door would have turned to splinters. It was already cracked open down the center.

Then he could hear the laughing of hyenas. Sounded like it. Maybe they weren't wolves out there after all.

"What's going on?"

Jonas nearly stepped forward to investigate before he remembered there was someone small and fragile in his arms, so he pulled back, letting Jackson do the investigating for him.

"Taylor, seriously, take her."

"No. I can hold them off better than you can."

Jonas couldn't make a decent argument with her in the limited time they had. What was he supposed to say? That he didn't trust himself not to drop his own daughter? That wouldn't go off very well.

Jackson glanced through the cracks of the door, his eyes flying wide before he looked back at Jonas.

No, not Jonas. He looked at Meg.

"We need to get out of here right now."

"What? Why? Can't we fight our way out?" Link asked.

"Not with gasoline."

Jonas got it. Taylor got it when she looked at him. "They can't!"

"They are."

They didn't have time for this. "Taylor, come with me and come with your daughter."

He could already smell the gasoline. The laughter had gotten louder. Someone outside shouted something. Jonas couldn't make it out with all the commotion inside, but he didn't think whatever was being yelled was directed at him.

"Taylor, do not fight me on this. We don't have time for that."

She glared at him. If he hadn't been holding onto their daughter, Jonas might have had reason to worry that she would get her inner bear out here and go on the attack.

And he wanted her to go on that attack more than she knew.

But not now. Definitely not now.

"We create the distraction. You all run, understand?" Steve asked.

Zelda's dark tail bristled. "Wait, what?"

They didn't give any more time to explain or plan. Link looked terrified to hell, but he still ran behind the other two, roaring with them as they burst through the door.

And then Jonas really could smell the gas. The sudden burst of flames that appeared right after was near blinding.

"Fuck!" Jonas pulled back from the fire.

For the first time in his adult life, since making it his career, fire had him at a disadvantage. Unprepared. Cornered.

He didn't have any of his gear, but he knew he could still manage this. He could do this for his daughter.

"Jackson, give Taylor your gun." Jackson did so. With Taylor armed, she wouldn't need to go into bear form, and he'd hopefully keep her with him. Next, he put Meg down on the floor and ripped the blankets off the bed. "Help me tie this," he told Taylor, as he stripped off his jacket and fashioned the top sheet into a sling for his busted arm. She helped him, and then picked Meg back up and pushed her into his good arm. He pulled his jacket over Meg. He didn't want a lick of flames on her. Or any of the smoke to get into her tiny lungs.

"We have to be fast about this. Got it?" He yelled at Taylor over the sound of the flames.

The fire ate the room around them quickly. It was hungry and alive, reaching for him and his child. But he would protect her.

He held his jacket over Meg's little body, tucking her chubby legs up and beneath it before he rushed towards the sounds of laughing outside, to the heat, to the fire.

CHAPTER 24

Taylor thought her heart damn near stopped for a second as she watched Jonas run towards the fire. It had already started eating its way into the room, crawling along the carpet and walls. The curtains were in flames.

It moved faster than she thought it would, but Jonas was outside of it now, with Meg.

Meg was safe. At least from the flames. Her baby girl was out there, which meant she needed to hurry and follow and face their attackers.

Taylor moved.

It was scary. More so than she would have thought jumping through something that was basically a ring of fire. Hotter, too. She was disoriented when she made it into the air outside that felt oddly cold against the heat of the fire.

The shouting and growling of the wolves around her came second. She spotted Link, doing his best in his fox shape to hold back the attacking. It was a flurry of fur, but none of the wolves paid any attention to her. Now that they had Steve and the others, they were less interested in Taylor and Jonas.

Zelda's car was trashed. Turned onto its side, windows smashed. She didn't have to use too much brain power to realize how that happened.

If her daughter weren't here, she would have tried to join the fight, to help fight those who'd caused her sloth and family so much trouble. But her daughter was here, and her priority was getting them to safety, as far away from the fire as possible.

Taylor glanced back at the door, to see if Zelda was getting ready to join her. When the fox jumped out, small and graceful, not a single flame marring that perfect fur, the group of fighting shifters was already taking their scuffle into the woods, away from the fire and away from the non-shifters inside.

Taylor turned her back to them and ran in the direction of her mate and child. She would have been able to sniff both of them out even if she were still engulfed in the smoke and flames.

When she found them, Jonas had discarded his jacket and was trying to comfort a crying Meg while trying the handles of the vehicles in the lot. When he spotted her, he smiled. A smile that made her stomach and heart ache. He had soot on his face; his hair was a little singed. She could smell the burn.

But Meg...Meg looked entirely untouched by the fire. Or by anything remotely harmful. Even if she was currently crying her eyes out, pushing against Jonas to try to get away, as though he was the one who had caused her latest upset.

Taylor ran to her daughter. She couldn't stop herself.

Meg reached out for her, and Taylor gave the gun to Jonas before grabbing her little girl out of his arms.

She'd been able to hold herself back before, but now all that bravado was out the window.

"Did you get a car?"

"Not yet." Jonas checked another vehicle. The alarm went off.

Instead of being upset by that, Jonas seemed happy. "Yes!"

He went to another truck, banging his hands on the hood, and when that did nothing, he rocked a smaller vehicle, which also had an alarm that started to blare.

"What are you doing? You'll call them right to us!"

"That's the point; I need to wake up the people here!" Jonas went to another vehicle, rocking it until the head-lights started to flash and the alarm sounded. "They can't be asleep with the fire going, and I can't go back to the building to find an alarm to pull."

Taylor blinked, looking up towards the windows on the first and second floor, which slowly began lighting up one by one. Shouting occurred from the people inside, as they tried to figure out what was going on.

Several loud yells of "Shut the fuck up!" or "Cut that shit out!" sounded from the doors and windows of the various rooms.

"Fire!" Jonas shouted, pointing toward the other side of the building, around the corner where they wouldn't be able to see it. "Evacuate the building right now! Leave everything behind. Do not pack your things and exit the premises!"

He sounded so official when he gave his instructions

to the people up there. Taylor pressed her lips together, watching as some of them started gathering up their things, not just their loved ones.

"Hurry up and get out!" She yelled. The few that were already down pulled out their phones. Some ran around to get video footage of the side of the building that was on fire. "You, call nine-one-one!" She'd seen Jonas do it before in the hotel room, but it would help to make sure someone got through to talk to the operator. The woman she'd pointed to did as she was told, stopping filming and pulling up her phone's keypad to dial instead. After what happened with her local fire department, Taylor figured anyone driving in would be whatever volunteers were left over, or maybe even from Astrea.

"People, don't stop here in the parking lot, keep moving. Get across the street. Do not stop." Jonas ushered the people as they ran around from the motel. A couple of small families. A few that looked like day hikers and some random people sprinkled into the mix who were probably just passing through and needed a place to stay for the night in between their travels.

Or to hide their affairs.

Despite Jonas' instructions, many of them had their bags and suitcases with them.

Taylor saw a kid with platinum blond hair, still standing around and filming the fires instead of getting to safety. His pupils were huge, and he smelled like something he was too young to be smoking. He looked too young to be around here, period.

"Give me your phone."

He frowned at her. "Fuck off, no way."

Taylor expected this, which was why she was calm when she let her claws and teeth make an appearance.

"What the fuck!"

The kid tried to step back, but the crowd of people moving through the parking lot was too thick. She was able to grab him by the scruff of his dirty hoodie before he could get far.

She didn't yank him too close. She didn't want him any closer than an arm's length anyway when she had her daughter in her arms. "You will give me your phone right now, or I will cut you." She let her eyes change. That always freaked out the non-shifters. They hated seeing that sort of thing directed at them. "Do you understand me?"

The boy trembled. He didn't piss himself, though, which was at least something. His hand did shake a little as he handed over his phone.

"Thank you."

Between the call from Jonas and the call from the lady she directed, Taylor hoped help was on the way already, but it couldn't hurt to give it one more go.

She dialed, got the operator, and told them exactly where she was and what was happening just in case they needed more information. Taylor didn't bother with staying on the line when the woman on the other end told her to though. She had other matters to attend to.

She called Andrew's home phone number, hoping someone would answer. If he'd managed to survive, he could have made it home by then.

"Come on, come on."

Thankfully, Jonas jogged towards her with a broad

smile on his face He'd managed to find a fire extinguisher, and, of all things, an ax.

She supposed that would be his weapon of choice, given the present situation.

He grinned from ear to ear. "I found another gun."

She blinked. "That's great. Uh, was it his?" Behind Jonas, a middle-aged man wearing a black shirt with the motel's logo on it walked, slowly taking in everything around him. He stared up at the growing flames, struck dumb as though he'd never seen anything quite like it.

To be fair, he probably hadn't ever seen his place of employment go up before. If he was the owner, then Taylor hoped he had insurance.

"He came out with some keys too, let's see which car they're for. Don't think he'll notice if we take a company car, do you?" The man was still staring, but had also followed the direction Jonas shoved him in, making his way out the parking lot and across the street with the others. He was the last one of the evacuees that Taylor could see.

She could kiss Jonas right then. She would later. When it was safe to do so. When she wasn't listening to the phone ringing endlessly as she prayed for Andrew to pick up. "Even better."

"I think they're for that truck over there," he pointed towards a truck with a large sticker promoting the hotel's name and number.

As she headed to the truck, someone finally answered on the phone.

It was Trevor, and he sounded uncertain and a little shaky. "Andrew's office."

Taylor knew exploded as Jonas unlocked the passenger

side door for her. "Trevor, you massive sack of…you had better have a good reason why you did what you did."

"Taylor?"

"No effing shit, moron!" She could only stop herself from swearing so much, even in front of her child. She was trying, however, which was way more than Trevor deserved.

"You are so lucky I've got my kid in my arms otherwise I'd let you have it. You betrayed us! You disgusting little maggot! I'm going to find you and make you regret this until your last breath, do you understand me?"

Jonas opened the truck door for her, grinning. "Just get in and drive," she muttered. Taylor didn't need to see him smirking at her over her foul mouth right then. She just wanted to cuss Trevor out, guilt-free, and get everything she could off her chest.

She put Meg in first, then climbed in after her. "You seriously think I had much choice?" Trevor's objections were meaningless to her.

"Screw you, weasel shifter, of course, you did. You never liked Jonas, and you were always looking for a reason to prop yourself up."

"I wasn't! All right?"

"Bullshit!"

"Bullshit," Meg repeated, though in a much calmer voice.

Taylor closed her eyes, begged for patience while Jonas still stood outside the truck.

"What are you doing?"

Jonas' gaze was directed back at the burning building. He couldn't seem to take his eyes away from it. "I need to make sure it's empty before we leave."

"What?"

"I'm sorry, I thought I could leave with you two, but you're going to have to hop over there and drive yourself and Meg to safety." He shook his head, and leaned down into the truck, placing his forehead on hers. "I can't leave people in need. But I need you two to get far away from here, from this fire and from the wolves who could decide to come back and finish the job." He reached for her with his good arm and pulled her him, letting their lips speak for everything left unsaid. Then, without another word, he placed the keys in her hand and walked away. He just tucked the ax into the back of his makeshift sling, grabbed the fire extinguisher, and ran back to the motel.

Taylor got out of the truck, pulling Meg along with her. There was no way she was going to drive out of there, past that crowd of people, knowing Jonas could die trying to be a hero. Even with the fire station so close around these parts, some of the volunteers lived far enough away that it would take time to round them up. She hoped they would be there soon to help Jonas, but she'd never be able to live knowing that she just left him.

Now that she was out of the truck, she saw that a few people had made their way back to the parking lot, and they were pointing up at the second floor. The group of teenagers gestured when Jonas went to talk to them.

That was why he'd rushed out of the truck. He'd seen what they were doing. More than just looking up at the growing flames. They'd been screaming out for one of their friends, and he, or she, was not making an appearance.

Taylor watched Jonas nod, and grab a water bottle from one of the teens before he ran for the stairs of the building that was half up in flames. She couldn't take her eyes off of him. She could barely hear Trevor on the other end of the line.

"These guys are crazy. You don't say no to that shit when it comes knocking, Taylor."

"Uh huh, well you can tell that to Andrew when you meet him."

She didn't explain what she meant by that when she hung up the phone.

Taylor was too busy watching Jonas working, fixated on him.

This was his life. This was what he did as a profession.

And goddamn, holding his child in her arms while watching him brave the flames was simultaneously the sexiest and most terrifying thing she had ever seen in her entire life.

"Go get 'em, tiger."

CHAPTER 25

It was differing being among the flames when he didn't have his gear. Not so much as an air tank. Jonas' body was exposed without the added weight, but someone was up here, and he didn't have a choice but to try to help them.

Those kids had been pointing and screaming towards this part of the building. When he'd asked, they said their friend had not met them at the muster point. He gave them instructions to get back over to safety and told them he'd do his best to find their friend.

The fire moved quickly. The heat more intense than he was comfortable with, that was for damned sure.

Jonas kept low. He wasn't in an enclosed space, which meant he had a better chance of avoiding too much smoke inhalation. The path was littered with discarded items, dropped when the occupants had fled for safety. Luckily, he found an abandoned shirt, so he didn't have to use his own. He grabbed the bit of cloth, soaked it with the water bottle contents, and wrapped the material around his face.

He spilled some of the remaining water on his shoulders and chest, and let some more splash down his back. It would make his clothes less flammable.

Using the fire extinguisher, Jonas sprayed the path ahead and below, to the fire licking up through the wooden planks.

He'd done this drill a thousand times before. He didn't have to put it out. He just needed to clear a path for himself and keep it open so he could walk back out again. There was no debris to clear, but the walkway wouldn't hold for much longer. He had to move.

He sprayed around the flooring where he walked. He had no idea how much of the extinguishing agent was inside of the container, so he had to move as quickly as possible. It looked old, so he couldn't rely on it to last long.

Not to mention this was absolutely not what he was supposed to be using for a fire this size.

Thankfully, the wind was with him. For now. It was a simple matter of getting to the room. It was one of the few where the door was still closed, and they'd told him what room number to look for.

The fire licked at the door, but it hadn't caught yet.

Jonas hung the fire extinguisher from the bottom of his sling and pulled the ax out from where he'd tucked it in the material behind him. "If you can hear me, stand back!" He shouted as loud as he could, and waited just a beat before swinging the ax with his good arm, splitting it before he kicked it down.

Smoke billowed out. He ducked down quickly, moving into the dark space.

* * *

TAYLOR WATCHED with the same intensity and focus as the people standing around her. She hated them at the moment. The people who pointed, stared with their mouths open, catching flies. Even the ones who were filming it.

She felt a mixture of hatred and sympathy for the people who were worried about their friend. On the one hand, their friend was missing. On the other, if they'd bothered to check on their friend when they were so concerned with packing their bags and getting themselves and their things to safety, then Jonas might not be risking his life right now.

She wanted Jonas to come out of there, get back down here, and be safe.

"He does this for a living. Daddy's going to be fine." Taylor repeated this mantra to Meg but knew she was saying it to try to calm herself more than the toddler. Meg knew that everything was chaos and that they were surrounded by panicked people, but she didn't understand what Jonas was facing.

"He does this for a living. He knows what he's doing." But firefighters also tended to have proper equipment and outerwear before they went into burning buildings.

"MAMAMA." Meg grabbed a handful of Taylor's hair, sighed, and put her face into her neck.

"He'll be back soon." Where the fuck was he? The seconds ticked by, each lasting a lifetime as she waited to see any movement in the cloud of black smoke.

Taylor nearly jumped out of her skin when a dark figure finally emerged from the smoke. Her heart leaped.

And then it froze in her throat.

Jonas was struggling. The protection she'd watched him put around his face was gone, and his face was black and soot. He moved much too slowly for her taste, and as he made his way through the smoke towards the stairs, she could make out that he had something around his shoulders.

Someone.

With his good arm, he'd managed to get the person over his shoulders. He had that arm wrapped around the person's and then secured across his chest, holding on to the person's arm that was draped over his opposite shoulder. Taylor heard Jonas cough and watched him stumble, but he kept moving forward.

When they disappeared into the stairwell, Taylor snapped out of it. She looked towards the person's friends. "Get over there! As soon as they come away from that building you take your friend so I can take care of mine!" She took off, running back across the street, but not going too close. She'd never forgive herself if she let something happen to him, but she still couldn't put Meg any closer.

The teens came with her, looking ready to run as soon as Jonas and their friend appeared. "Carol! Carol, come on," they cheered, as Taylor held an arm back to stop them from running too close and putting themselves in danger.

She sure as hell would be right there with Jonas if it weren't for Meg.

Jonas' figure emerged from the smoke and fire, moving even slower. "Come on baby, just a few more steps!" Taylor joined in the chanting. When she couldn't wait any longer and got ready to run to him, three men ran past her and the teens. One pulled the girl, Carol, off Jonas' shoulders and put her on his own. The other two helped Jonas, who was almost unable to stand with how hard he was coughing.

Away from the fire and off the parking lot, onto softer dirt and grass across the street, the woman's friends clustered around her like hummingbirds searching for sugar. "Give her a chance to breathe," Jonas said while trying to breath himself.

"What about you?" She was more concerned about her mate than she was this stranger. Taylor didn't care how heartless that made her either.

"I'll be fine. She needs more help." He wasn't coughing anymore, which was good, but his preoccupation with the woman on the ground worried Taylor. She knew she'd have to step up and care for the woman if she wanted Jonas to sit back and let his sub-human strength heal him faster.

"What do we do?" One of Carol's friends cried.

"Is she alive?" The other moaned.

Taylor had taken basic first aid courses but had never had to use any of her skills. After her freeze up at the fire station, she didn't know if she'd ever be able to. Taylor didn't like this feeling. She didn't like that her brain struggled to think of what to do in this situation.

She thought about Andrew, and how she wished she'd had a chance to help him, but she made herself focus. Right now, it was this girl, and no one else was volunteering to help.

"I know first aid." She said, making her way over. "Do

either of you?" One of the girls shook her head, the other shrugged — one of the men who'd helped raised his hand.

Taylor looked at Meg in her arms for a moment. She didn't feel safe letting her go, but she couldn't leave her with Jonas, who was too covered in smoke to be healthy for a baby. Finally, she handed Meg over to one of the girls. "I'm going to help your friend, but don't you dare take a step away from me, or momma bear mode is going to come out. It's been a long day, so don't test me." The girl gulped, but nodded and took Meg.

Taylor got down on her hands and knees, by Carol's face. She pointed to the man. "You, do the chest compressions. I'll do the air."

"Check her pupils." Jonas wheezed from a few feet away. "And her airways."

"Right." Taylor did as he instructed, and when she confirmed the airways were clear she nodded to the man, and they began alternating chest compressions and mouth-to-mouth.

When the woman inhaled a sharp breath, a cheer went up. Taylor backed up to give her room to turn on her side and cough. Her friends came closer, the one handing Meg back to Taylor.

Relief washed over Taylor, and she turned back to assess Jonas fully. She went to him, hesitant to touch him. "Are you okay? Do you need a hospital?"

She didn't see any burns on him. Didn't smell any blood, but that didn't mean everything was all right.

"I'm fine."

"Are you sure? Don't give me this tough guy bullshit."

Even now she could see he was taking deep breaths

and looking close to the sun to make his eyes water and rinse out the smoke and ash.

"The fire didn't make it into the room. It was just a lot of smoke and heat. Fuck."

Taylor looked at the crowd of people. "Anyone else have another water bottle?"

Preferably sealed.

Luckily, someone had salvaged a cooler full of ice and water from their vehicle. They handed bottles over for Carol and Jonas.

"Tilt your head back."

He did. Taylor couldn't be as careful as she wanted to, so she ended up spilling some of the water down his face and chest, but when he sighed, opening his eyes to the liquid, she knew it didn't matter.

"We still have to get out of here," she said. "The wolves are still in the area."

"Can you still smell them close by?"

That was the problem. She could. "Yeah, but I don't hear the fighting anymore."

Jonas stood up, shaking his hair out and spraying water as if he were a dog.

Some subhumans did keep a few baser animal instincts.

"That's not good."

"Should we stay? Emergency vehicles are almost here."

"Can you hear them?"

Taylor nodded. "Yeah. They're getting close."

She could make out the sounds of sirens in the distance. Realistically, it hadn't been that long since she'd called, but at the moment, with everything going on, it felt like a lifetime.

Jonas glanced around. "Right. We'll stick around, but we need to stay in the crowd."

Taylor nodded. There were people all around them, so there was no need to back off. The truck they had been about to steal wasn't exactly far away, but it was away from the crowd, and around the edge of dim light spilling down from one of the few parking lot lamps.

Not exactly a safe idea to go over there and risk something happening. It would be just asking for someone to grab either of them from the darkness and make their kill.

By the time the firefighters, police, and ambulance arrived, the whole motel burned bright. Maybe half the building could be saved. Maybe. Taylor didn't know much about these things.

When Taylor looked at Jonas, she could see a whole different kind of fire in his eyes. He wanted to join them. He wanted to suit up and handle the hose.

And Taylor was so damned proud of him.

She recognized Detective Grey. His suit looked a touch disheveled as he pulled the jacket back to survey the scene.

"You still have the gun?"

"Yeah, right here."

"Give it to me."

Jonas took it, slipping it into the back waist of his pants with a slight wince. "Don't have a permit, and I don't want to deal with this right now. Let's go and talk to him."

Taylor took Jonas' hand, holding it tightly as they moved.

Jonas still felt a little too warm after being in that building.

They got the detective's attention before the man could move on. He didn't exactly look happy to see either of them.

"What the hell is going on here?"

"The wolves attacked us," Jonas said. "They might have killed her alpha; his truck should be on the side of the main highway leading up to the local bear sloth. A dead wolf should be on the highway. We were brought here, more wolves came, and they lit the place up with gas. This is a revenge thing. The alpha is angry because his brother tried to go after a conduit, and the conduit's mate tortured him for the effort."

Wow. He wasted no time. Taylor nodded. "Yeah, all of that."

Grey looked at her. "You're alpha might be dead?"

It knifed her every time she heard it. "Yeah."

But she hoped he wasn't. God, she was really hoping Andrew was alive.

"All right, give me a second." Grey pulled his radio out. He seemed to be sending instructions out to the other officers around the area. He told them to do a sweep around the motel itself to search for signs of fighting before he turned his attention back to Taylor and Jonas.

"Do you know if anyone is in there?"

"He got everyone out that he could," Taylor said quickly.

"There was a girl passed out on the second floor; I got her out."

"Which is why you look like this? All right, where is she?"

Jonas pointed the way, and Grey made sure the paramedics knew where to go to take care of her before he turned his attention back to Jonas.

"You all right? I know you're subhuman, but say the word, and I'll get someone over here to look you over, all right?"

"I don't need anything other than getting Taylor and my daughter somewhere safe until you can get the cops up to her sloth to take care of the shit that's infested it."

Taylor heard the growl in his voice. Either from being called subhuman, or from the pile-up of everything that had happened, she couldn't be sure, and it didn't matter.

"I can take you to the station. And I'll call someone to get some stuff to help with the little one."

With the sound of all the sirens, Meg had started shrieking a song of painful death in Taylor's ear. Her diaper felt and smelled awful, she hadn't eaten since she'd been with Andrew, and as of right now, her mother was completely done with everything.

Taylor wanted to take care of her daughter, somewhere safe where she could see Jonas and Meg at the same time while knowing something was being done about the wolves.

"Thank you."

"Come on, we can take my car," Grey said.

Before they could get there, a fox landed heavily onto the hood. Screams sounded as a man followed. He jumped up high, landing on the front hood with such force that the front tires burst, and leaving no doubt that the engine was totaled after something like that.

The screaming started. Civilians began to move, the police drew their guns, but it was too late.

CHAPTER 26

Jonas grabbed Taylor's shoulders, putting his body over top of her and their daughter when the first shots were fired.

Knowing any one of those popping sounds could hit Jonas, could hit their child, made Taylor's heart leap, and her lungs constrict. She couldn't breathe. She couldn't think.

No, she couldn't breathe because Jonas' weight was on top of her. Meg cried and screamed her little lungs out, so she clearly still had room to inhale lots of air.

Taylor swiftly ran her hands over her daughter's body, searching for signs of any wounds, anything that would indicate an injury.

She felt nothing warm and wet, other than her diaper, and she smelled no blood. Meg was fine. The gunfire had stopped.

"Are you all right?"

Taylor nodded, carefully peaking over Jonas' shoulder. "I don't see them."

"They're around."

She knew it, too. She could smell the wolves. They were close.

The chaos would start again soon. Jonas carefully pulled himself off of Taylor's body. He looked around; his eyes were alert while the fire blazed high and bright behind him.

He looked as though he was engulfed in the fire, as though it was already part of him. A man on fire who would protect his daughter, and her. Even though he didn't have the same superhuman strength that they had.

Taylor grabbed him by the back of the neck, ignoring the startled expression on his face as she dragged him down and crushed her mouth to his.

She kissed him. Long and sweet. His mouth softened against hers, eventually, but it didn't last for long before they had to pull back from each other.

"We have to go." Jonas pulled himself up, held out his hand.

Taylor didn't hesitate to take it. "Right."

Jonas yanked her up. He was stronger than she remembered. Taylor couldn't pinpoint exactly what it was. At that moment, he seemed like the most powerful man in the world.

"Grey!"

Jonas started running. Detective Grey had taken cover behind one of the cruisers. He clutched at his side, his face pale. Other officers were down. Three more worked to subdue one of the wolves, striking it again and again with their Tasers when it wouldn't stay down. It looked like they weren't taking any risks with their lives now that some of their friends weren't moving.

Jonas made it to Grey quickly. Taylor knelt with him, but only because she didn't trust herself to remain standing when there were people out there trying to get a look at who to attack next.

"Is it bad?"

"Just a scratch. It better be." Grey clenched his teeth.

Taylor shook her head. "You look like you're in pain. You need a paramedic." She looked up and called out, "Someone help! There's an officer down over here!"

That's what people said when it was a cop who had been injured, right?

"It's fine." Grey grinned, though it looked massively forced under the strain. "It's good to feel pain. If I didn't feel it, I'd be worried. Might think I was dying."

Taylor wasn't sure if that was true or not, and this man was a human. He wouldn't have the healing abilities of a shifter. Or the healing abilities of a mated subhuman.

She glanced at Jonas.

"I don't think they're after you. Not specifically," Grey said through clenched teeth. "They want to get back at Steve and everyone connected to him. There was an attack at the hospital. They tried to get Victor. Didn't work. We were waiting."

"Victor. Zelda's mate." Taylor was still trying to get the names right of all these people. People she didn't know, but whose actions put herself, her sloth, her mate, and her daughter at risk.

Grey nodded. "Yeah. Look, take my car, if it will run." He reached into his pocket with a pained grunt, pulling out his keys. "Get to the station, hide there, wait for everything to blow over and—"

Grey's words were cut short when, not a wolf, but a

bear reached around from the top of the car, grabbed him by the top of his head and yanked him clean off the ground.

It threw him away so casually, Grey screamed, but the bear just looked at them.

And Taylor wanted to kill him.

"Trevor! You asshole! What are you doing?"

The bear looked down at her, its eyes popping wide like a puppy kicked for no reason.

He wasn't in a standard bear shape. She hadn't even known he could do this, but she could smell it all over him who this was. It wasn't just in the shape and color of his eyes or the off patches of fur that grew out in shaggy, mismatched directions.

"Do you have any idea what the fuck you're doing? Look at these people!"

She pointed around at the chaos, the people who were down. Several people looked over towards them. The few officers who were still standing brought out their weapons. They had the guns pointed in the right direction, but they seemed unsure, as if all the injured around them were a warning for what would happen to them next.

In his in-between form, Trevor had enough of his original form that he was able to use his voice box, even in this monstrous shape.

"Give them what they want, they go away."

She sneered at him. "They killed Andrew, you know."

Trevor's eyes flew wide. He stared at her, his jaw falling, revealing sharp fangs.

To the officers standing around, he probably looked

more menacing than shocked, which was likely why they straightened their backs, shouting out to him.

"You! Get back into your natural shape right now, or we will open fire!"

Trevor stared at her as Taylor continued to back up. Jonas moved with her, though he stayed in front, shielding her and Meg.

"You did this, Trevor. You brought them here, and now everything is going to shit. Give yourself up."

Trevor growled, his snout crinkling as the deep rumble vibrated up through his chest.

The police were losing their patience as well. "This is your last warning! Turn back into your natural form, or we will open fire on you!"

Trevor growled at Jonas. His eyes glowed that of a creature that was angry, that wanted revenge.

Jonas shook his head. "Don't even think about it."

Trevor did think about it. If Taylor didn't have Meg in her arms, she could have done something, something other than let herself be shoved backward by Jonas as Trevor snapped his teeth around Jonas' shoulder and middle.

Jonas screamed from the pain of being bitten. Taylor backed up, part of her screaming that she needed to get into her bear shape and defend him, and the other part of refusing to let her forget she was holding onto something so much more precious in her arms.

"Trevor! Stop!"

"Hold your fire!"

The police opted not to shoot now that the giant bear thing had a victim in its mouth, but Trevor didn't shake

Jonas' body around until he stopped moving the way she expected him to.

Trevor turned, leaped neatly off the police cruiser, and darted into the shadows with Jonas, just out of reach of the fire and the motel lights.

No one gave chase because no one here could keep up with a shifter in a form like that.

Taylor could. Maybe those other shifters, Zelda, Steve, Link…

Well, she didn't know if Link was still alive or not, judging by the fact that his fox hadn't moved from where he landed on the car hood, but she had to do something.

"Grey! Detective Grey!"

She hoped he was alive. Prayed for him to be alive. There was no one else she would trust with this sort of task.

"Grey! Detective Grey!"

"Thankfully, he was already groaning and pushing himself onto his side, his face twisting with pain. He clearly wasn't having a good day.

"What the fucking hell—"

"Here. Take her."

"Wait, what? Hey! What the hell do you think you're doing?"

Taylor kissed her child on both of her cheeks, her hands aching to have to let her go, but she needed to move fast. "Keep her safe until I get back, all right?"

"Where the fuck are you going? Do I look like I can look after a little girl right now?"

"The paramedics will help you with that, just watch her! Please."

The detective yelled some more expletives at her,

words Meg definitely should not be hearing with her tender, innocent little bear ears, but there was nothing to be done for it. Someone took Taylor's man, and she needed to kick some ass here.

Taylor ran to the edge of the parking lot, where the lights didn't quite reach. She pumped her arms, smelling the wolves all around her as she ran into the trees, flying on the wind.

They were watching her. Maybe deciding when to move in?

Taylor let her claws out. If they tried to come up to her, then she would show them what a mother bear could really do what she was pissed off, and right now, Taylor was angry enough to topple some of the trees around her.

She moved fast, hard, ignoring the sting of branches slapping against her face, arms, and legs. It didn't matter because soon she didn't feel it anyway. She only felt the prickle of her snout changing. Fur sliding in through her pores like thousands of tiny needles.

She no longer had to hold back the bear inside her, and if Trevor hurt Jonas, if he did irreparable damage, or worse...

She'd send Trevor to meet Andrew much sooner than expected, but with a lot more pain.

CHAPTER 27

*J*onas had no idea where Trevor was taking him for the first minute or so of his kidnapping.

But he figured it out when, twenty seconds after dragging Jonas into the woods, the other man didn't immediately tear him to pieces.

Trevor's bite didn't sink too deep, but deep enough that it fucking hurt, and now it was starting to burn.

Bite chasers would kill to be in Jonas' position right about now, but Jonas wasn't in the mood to risk his life so he could have the chance to turn into a shifter of any kind. He'd already been bitten by a wolf earlier, but it had only been enough to render his arm useless. Now Trevor was working on that same shoulder, and Jonas was losing feeling down that side of his body. The cold sensation that came after wasn't much of a good sign either.

Jonas pounded on Trevor's snout as hard as he could. He reached for his eyes but couldn't get his arm up that high with the awkward angle.

He was going to fuck Trevor up when he got the chance for this. If Trevor of all people was one of the assholes to kill him, then Jonas was going to be massively pissed.

"Trevor! Put me down!"

He'd left Taylor and Meg behind undefended. He needed to get back to them.

Or, no, maybe this was good. Maybe Trevor and the wolves would leave Taylor and Meg and the rest of the humans alone if they had him.

Still, that didn't mean Jonas was going to give up without some fight. Even if Taylor and Meg were safe—well, safer—where there were police, a crowd of people and paramedics, Jonas wasn't going to lie down and die without a proper fight.

He kept smashing his good fist against Trevor's nose.

Even in a bear shifter, that was still a pressure point. Some things were universal. Jonas felt the wince in the shifter every time his fist hit at just the right spot.

"Drop me. Let me go. Put me down. Come on!"

Eventually, Trevor could take no more. His golden eyes had started to water. He spat Jonas out, but Jonas wasn't nearly as fast as a shifter. Trevor grabbed him by his throat with his long, twisted fingers, his claws scraping against the back of his neck, yanking him close.

"Stop that!" Trevor's warm breath blew hot spittle into Jonas' face.

He forced a grin at the man. "You should look into brushing your teeth from time to time. I hear it does wonders for this sort of problem you're having."

Jonas could have sworn he saw blood vessels popping in Trevor's eyes. Enraged, he threw Jonas down onto the ground, his giant foot pressing down on his stomach.

The worst part was that Trevor wasn't even adding a lot of weight, but Jonas grunted under the pressure, holding tightly to his furry ankle, trying his best to keep Trevor's fat ass off him.

"Why did she pick you? Why did you come back?"

Jonas clenched his teeth, hardly able to get the words out. "Are you kidding me? Everything happening and you care about that? Your alpha is dead you sack of shit."

"Because you wouldn't leave well enough alone!" Trevor pointed a clawed finger down at him, and once again, Jonas had to wonder if he was out of his damned mind.

"They came here looking for the conduit. You knew that! You were trying to help them!"

"To get rid of them. They want revenge for their brethren. It's what any good pack would do. You would understand if you weren't a subhuman."

All of Jonas' anger, all of his hatred bubbled up to the surface. He pushed harder against the paw that held him down, sneering up at Trevor as he managed to get the man off him just a little.

Trevor pressed down harder. It hurt. The pain in his side was almost too much, and this couldn't be making it better, but Jonas was determined to keep Trevor's filthy paws off him.

Trevor bared his teeth, barking down at him, but then a very feminine, furious scream broke off whatever he was about to say.

"Let go of me you son of a bitch! I'll kill all of you!"

That wasn't Taylor, thank God, but it sounded like… the fox woman. Zelda.

Jonas took his attention away from Trevor for one second, one second too long, because the deformed bear thing reached down, grabbing Jonas by the throat before lifting him off his feet.

"I'll let them deal with you."

Them?

Trevor took Jonas towards the screaming. It wasn't far. Off the path they'd already been traveling, across a shallow stream, and up a small hill, to a small clearing.

It was dark, the moon shone down on them, but if it weren't for his enhanced eyesight, Jonas doubted he would be able to see much of anything that was going on.

Zelda was there. Her hair was disheveled. Her eyes blazed brightly through the dirt tracks on her face. Blood gleamed on her fingertips as she flew at the men and wolves surrounding her.

They dodged the swipes of her clawed hands with ease, laughing at her, as though it were some game.

Trevor threw Jonas down into the middle of the clearing between them. He grunted, the air shooting out his lungs the moment of impact.

Jonas clutched at his bleeding side, coughing for breath.

And suddenly, all that smoke he'd been fighting not to inhale when he went into that hot motel room seemed to shoot right into his lungs, despite being as far away from the fire as he could get.

Zelda shrieked something next to him, but she didn't sound as though she were in pain, or any real danger, so he ignored her and let her rant while he got control over himself again.

This was such bullshit. If Jonas ever got the chance, he was going to wring Trevor's stupid neck for this.

Jonas rolled to his knees, glancing up, noting how utterly out of control the wolves, and Trevor, seemed to have of Zelda.

She looked more like a wild banshee than a fox as she swung her small, clawed hands out at the wolves around her.

Jonas did a quick count. There were four wolves and Trevor. They seemed to have shifted themselves into the in-between form. They stood on their hind legs, had opposable thumbs, but their bodies looked to be, for the most part, that of wolves. Even their snouts and heads were more wolf-like than human. It was interesting to watch the way they avoided Zelda's claws. Some didn't get out of the way fast enough.

These were the guys who were burning down patches of forest, who burned down homes and business, and yet they avoided a woman much smaller than they were as though their principals refused to allow them to fight back.

They deflected her blows, some laughed over it, but none struck Zelda back.

One of the males eventually grabbed onto her wrists, making a show of how she couldn't get away from him.

It was weird watching a wolf making kissy faces at Zelda while she struggled to get away from him, taunting her as she shrieked at him.

Jonas couldn't take it. He pushed himself to his feet, flying at the wolf, catching the shifter off guard as he put all of his weight and power into the tackle. Shoving his good shoulder into the shifter's middle, he threw it off its feet. Its claws dug into Jonas' chest, trying to free itself.

Jonas had seen shifters fight before, and it was always a gruesome sight to behold. To be in one himself, and to be on top of a shifter while it fought and struggled to get away from him was something else entirely.

The shifter snapped its teeth at him, narrowly missing his face. Jonas managed to pin the arms of the shifter down with his feet. Even with subhuman strength, he only had one working arm, and it took everything he had to hold the beast. It was one hell of a ride as the wolf-man beneath him bucked and tried to roll.

Jonas slammed his fists down again and again on the side of the wolf's head, going for the eyes. He struck the wolf once hard on the nose. That seemed to do it. The wolf whined and turned subdued, looking away with the sudden strike against a pressure point.

Apparently, that was too much for the other wolves standing around, and for Trevor. They must have thought it was funny at first, watching the subhuman going at it with one of their own. But when it got clear their friend wouldn't win, they yanked Jonas away from him.

Jonas roared, pulling against their hands, their claws slicing into him even as he fought them. He cursed them and their mothers. He wanted blood. He couldn't think of anything other than how much he wanted to open their bellies up and let their guts spill out for what they were doing here. For what they'd done to Captain Burns. For what they'd done to Andrew and Grey, and for what they'd tried to do to Taylor and Meg.

Trevor was the guiltiest out of the lot of them. He'd

betrayed his sloth, even if he tried to justify it by saying he was trying to get rid of the wolves. Jonas didn't care anymore. He just wanted to crush the man's head in with his bare hands.

"Trevor! You fucking traitor!"

Trevor let out a little whining noise, his bear ears falling on top of his head and holding tightly to his skull, though he didn't say anything.

One of the wolves sucker punched him in the gut, knocking the wind out of him, again, before tossing him onto the ground.

"Stay down," it warned with its growly voice.

Zelda kneeled next to him, worry in her eyes for him before she glared back up at the others.

"If my brother is hurt, I swear I will skin all of you alive and turn you into rugs."

"Your brother…" Jonas thought about that. He'd seen the other fox, but he hadn't looked in a good position.

"Did you see him?"

Jonas thought the fox shifter was alive, but he didn't want to get into too many details with Zelda right now.

No point in worrying her any more.

Zelda sighed, but then she went back to sneering at the men around her, the fur of her tail bristling as she stood up.

"I didn't have anything to do with your stupid brother getting hurt, and I don't know anything about a conduit! You're attacking the wrong people!"

Wait, one of these guys was the brother?

The shifters around him were all around the same size and build, likely all alphas, but there was one that was a touch bigger, a bit wider around the shoulders. He shifted, shrinking down into his human shape.

Even like that, he was still over six feet tall. Maybe even taller than Jonas. That annoyed him.

The man pressed his lips together into a fine line. He put his hands behind his back, the way Jonas had seen cartoon villains do when he was still a kid watching those kinds of shows. He regarded Zelda with cold, unfeeling eyes. Dark eyes. Not the usual sort of dark, but this guy… looked as though a demon possessed him.

"You know the men who hurt my brother. They sent him back to me with strips of his skin missing." He approached slowly, his pace somehow more menacing than if he'd run at her. Zelda backed up. Jonas struggled to his feet, putting himself between the fox shifter and the crazy wolf before he could take another step towards her.

"That's as far as you go, pal."

The man regarded him. "Do you have family?"

He thought of Meg. Of Taylor. "Yeah, I do."

"Good. Then you know what you would do for them if someone were to tie any of them down, were to hurt them. I get the feeling that if I were to seek out that blue-haired bitch you were with and do half of what they did to my brother, you would try to tear me to pieces."

Jonas nodded. "You're right; I would. And you did come after her, so that's one thing. Two is that I doubt my mate and infant daughter would be tearing strips off of anyone in your family, and the third is that female bears aren't called bitches. That's what you would be."

Not the best come back he'd ever thought up. On a scale of one to amazing one-liners, it ranked up there with baby talk, a first timer trying to get a good one in, but it was enough to piss off the wolf in front of him, so when he backhanded Jonas hard enough to throw him into a tree, he had to admit, he didn't really mind it so much.

But only because he didn't feel the strike until well after impact.

By then, the wolf shifter had flown at him, his overly large, clawed hand wrapping around Jonas' throat, holding him up against the birch tree.

That did hurt. This guy wasn't just a normal shifter and had more than just the skill of shifting into an in-between form, something between man and wolf, or man and bear. He had more ability to control his body, his inner wolf, to the point where he could not only bring out his claws and change his eyes, but his entire hand around Jonas' throat felt different, rough and painful. It felt as though the wolf were choking the life out of him when an ordinary-looking, if not larger than average, man stood in front of him.

"This little bitch behind me is the mate of the man who is friends with the man who hurt my brother. You are part of the sloth that refused to help us get justice. You're the one who got the humans involved and a traitor to shifters everywhere."

"Great," Jonas had to choose his words carefully since he could hardly take in a breath to make them. "You gonna go after Zelda's second cousin, too? Maybe my co-worker's grandkids' friends' roommate for not helping you get revenge, too?"

The hand around his throat tightened. Jonas couldn't say a word after that, but as he gagged for breath, he was pretty sure that was something of the point.

"Wait! Wait, stop!" Zelda shouted. She tried to rush to him, but Trevor grabbed her arms. The three other wolves stepped in her way.

As Zelda kicked Trevor in the dick, Jonas was struck with guilt over the way he'd previously thought about her. She was kind of cool, but he still wished her family drama, or whatever this was, hadn't sucked Taylor of Meg into this.

Black started to close in around Jonas' line of vision. He was stunned to realize Trevor wasn't looking at him as though he were glad for this. The man was an asshole. He'd always had eyes for Taylor. The little peckerhead should be loving this.

Whatever. Jonas was dying. His face felt hotter than any fire, and he didn't care anymore.

He slammed his fist into the man's gut.

It didn't have the desired effect. The shifter kept holding onto him and barely grunted. Jonas wasted that precious oxygen trying to get this prick off him.

He slammed another fist into his gut. Then another. The wolf looked at him as though Jonas were punching at the air instead of his ribs. Each strike was weaker than the last.

"Don, I'm sure he understands now."

Was Trevor defending him?

"No, he doesn't understand."

Don? Not exactly the name Jonas expected from a fire-starting villain.

Those eyes glowed bright red, and they were all Jonas could see through the straw hole of his vision.

"Not yet."

Jonas sank into the darkness. He tried grabbing onto

Don's arm, to make one last effort to pull the man off, but his fingers touched air as he slumped. It was actually kind of peaceful. He'd just let himself go under before coming back strong.

Yeah, this wasn't over. He was just letting Don think it was done. Jonas just needed to sleep first.

CHAPTER 28

The sinking feeling stayed with Jonas for what felt like hours, until it was no longer a sinking feeling. Now it was just a feeling of dropping.

Down, down, down. Until he slammed hard onto the pavement, through the pavement, bursting through layers of Earth's crust, his body smashing into paste.

Jonas gasped hard, pushing himself up onto his hands and rolling to the side, coughing for breath, the pain in his side almost too much for him to handle as he sucked back precious air.

He wasn't on the road, he hadn't smashed through the pavement, and his body wasn't a pudding of his flesh on impact.

He was still out in the woods. It was still dark except for the moon shining down on him, and he could still hear Zelda going at it with the wolves behind him.

No, not Zelda. Foxes didn't make that sort of deep, skin-tingling roar.

Jonas raised his face, still heated from a lack of blood

231

flow, taking note of the black bear with gleaming blue fur taking swipes at the wolves that surrounded her.

And she was vicious.

Much as it was Jonas' first instinct to be horrified that Taylor was fighting, outnumbered, a group of wolves like this, he couldn't help but admire the way she went at her enemies.

Even outnumbered, she somehow managed to push them back. She kept them on their toes, but they were ruthless. The instant one jumped onto her back and started biting at her neck, Jonas flew into action.

He grabbed the nearest thing he could get his hand on, which was a large, awkward-looking stick.

He would have rather had a rock at that moment, but this did just as well when he came up to the side of his mate's body, jabbing the business end of the stick hard against the side of the wolf's face.

He narrowly missed its eye, but it didn't appear as though that made the strike hurt any less as the wolf cried out and sharply fell off Taylor's back.

The reactions of anyone or anything trying to protect their eyes always tended to border on the extreme.

Another wolf came. Not the biggest one, so it wasn't Don, but Jonas lifted his stick high, wishing he had his ax as he swung it down hard across the side of the wolf's face.

It snapped his stick in half, but at least he now had a much pointier side to work with.

He could use that. He was going to use it.

"Come on! Come and get me!"

Jonas ducked down when he felt something moving

behind him, turning just in time to see a dark fox had jumped onto one of the wolves.

Zelda struggled to keep it off her once the tables were turned, kicking her legs up, two sets of teeth snapping at each other.

She didn't stand a chance, but then Jonas barely managed to pull his hand back before it was bitten right off by another snapping wolf.

This one was a big one. Had to be Don.

Jonas lifted his broken stick, holding it as he would a vampire stake. "I will fuck you up if you think about coming near her."

Not that he could do much about it considering two of the other wolves were already giving Taylor trouble. Trevor continued to stand off to the side, being a useless asshole, probably waiting to find out for sure who would win before he jumped in to help.

"I just want the wolf that hurt my brother."

Jones jerked back, stunned the guy could control his shifting ability that well that he could talk while in full wolf form.

Whatever. Jonas didn't have time for this. "She didn't have anything to do with that, neither did Andrew."

"Andrew got in my way. He refused to help. Even a subhuman like you knows shifters watch out for each other. Even a subhuman should know that we take care of our own."

"Yeah, well, the law has something else to say about that."

It was the wrong thing to say. Don flew at him. Jonas barely managed to duck out of the way the first time.

"I'll crush your head between my teeth!"

Jonas nodded. "Yeah, probably, but you're going to have to work for that privilege."

The wolf lunged for him again. Jonas couldn't bring himself to get out of the way fast enough. Don crashed into him.

Jonas brought up his arm, the stake in hand.

The bite on his arm burned. The stake was piercing his own hand as it went through the thick fur around Don's neck.

He knew he'd made it through the protective fur when the wolf screamed out in pain, pulling back.

There was blood at the pointed end of the stake. Jonas looked at it, and the wolf as it staggered back.

But it didn't seem to be enough to take Don down. The wolf stumbled, but it looked at him with bright red eyes.

"You motherfucker," Don growled, his voice sounded as though air bubbles were bursting within it.

Meanwhile, Jonas' arm trembled and felt cold as all hell as he pushed himself back.

He had so many holes in him right now it was a small miracle he was still conscious.

Too bad that miracle wasn't enough to keep Don down. If the damned fleabag hadn't been determined to get him before, then he was right now.

Jonas looked over to Taylor. She was still standing, still holding her own. He hoped it stayed that way and this wouldn't distract her.

He just wished…

Don squared himself, his shoulder bunching as he crouched low before leaping at Jonas one more time.

Those teeth, the warm breath, and spittle that got so close Jonas could see the reflection of his face in it, didn't get the chance to touch him as another bear, a huge brown bear, crashed into Don before he could make his kill.

Jonas blinked. Then he breathed, noting the way the two shifters went at it, and this time it was something else. An actual fight to the death, but one dog happened to be three times the size of the other, and the other was a bear and was already injured.

Andrew.

Jonas sucked back a heavy breath, dragging himself back to the trees, somewhere he could prop himself up. His arm killed, and his side...he didn't even want to think about it, but fuck him sideways. Andrew was alive. He was here.

Which meant Taylor and Zelda had a chance.

He looked back to his mate, and Jonas blinked again, wondering how high he was on adrenaline when he spotted two more wolves helping with the fight.

Steve and Jackson? Had to be. Don's men wouldn't be helping Taylor or Zelda, and the smell was...well, he had trouble smelling anything while caked in his own blood, and his sense of smell was shit compared to an actual shifter, to begin with, but he was getting hints of those other wolves in the air, so he was pretty sure it was them.

Not that it meant he could relax. His body screamed for him to let the others take control now that they were here, but his heart and soul couldn't lie back and do nothing while Taylor continued to fight.

But his body was so damned heavy...

Why were the woods swirling around like that? Jonas blinked a couple of times, trying to keep himself awake, but it wasn't just the need for sleep that was getting to him.

He glanced towards a sound in the trees. He spotted Trevor. Hiding.

A growl worked its way up Jonas' throat. He dug his fingers into the dirt, wanting to go after him, to strangle the bastard for his part in this. Jonas didn't care about his reasoning.

Trevor, even in his bear shape, somehow managed to look a little scared before he turned tail and made a run for it.

Really? That was it? Even when Jonas looked like this, when he felt like this, Trevor ran from him?

Damned pussy.

Jonas searched for something he could use, anything that would help him if someone walked up to him, or tried going for Taylor while her back was turned. He found a rock. It had a slight point. It was dull, but it was good enough.

He kept his eye on the black bear, watching as she roared and slashed out her claws, chasing away. And he was so fucking proud of her.

She was the one. The one he wanted to spend the rest of his life with. If he got a life after this.

He was so fucking stupid to have left her behind. So stupid…

At some point, Taylor noticed him. Maybe it was the way he'd been staring at the back of her head. It was difficult to say, but if a bear could have a terrified look on its face, then Taylor managed to pull it off.

The bear rushed to him, shrinking down, transforming into the sexy bombshell Jonas knew and loved.

Taylor didn't look as happy as Jonas felt when she put her hands onto his cheeks.

She looked as though someone had just run over her dog in front of her. Not that she had a dog, but the idea was the same.

"Oh God, Jonas, baby."

"I'm good."

He touched her wrist. His hand was wet. Was he sitting in a puddle?

"You're not all right! Steve! Jackson!"

What did she think they were going to do?

"Where's Meg?"

Taylor shook her head. "I...I left her with Detective Grey. She's fine. She's safe."

Her eyes were shining. Not just because they were fantastic eyes to look at either. They shone as though she were trying not to cry. Jonas didn't like that. "Did they hurt you? Did Trevor...?"

"No, no, try not to talk so much. You'll be all right." She looked at his arm, then his stomach, her face twisting. "Oh, God..."

That didn't sound so great, and while Jonas knew he should be worried, he felt strangely at peace with this. He was pretty sure Taylor was scared he was going to die, but going out fighting, after doing his job one last time, and helping to take out the wolves that had been starting these fires, protecting his woman and his child, felt pretty good.

It would have been nice to get to know Meg, to watch her grow up, but she would get to grow up, that was better than getting to know her.

Jackson clouded his view by standing over him and Taylor. The man's chest was bare. Slash marks ran down his skin, and his ear looked mangled to all hell, but otherwise, he was stoic as he knelt.

"He needs treatment. He still has a chance, but a human isn't made for this sort of punishment."

"He's not just a human. He's one of us! A subhuman. He can handle it, right, Jonas?"

Only she could make the word subhuman sound like a compliment. Not just a compliment, but a benefit. He loved her so much for that.

She touched his face, Jonas liked that, too, but he didn't like it so much when she gently slapped at his cheeks.

"Don't do that, stay awake."

"Right," he said, forcing his eyes open, and it got a little easier for him to keep them open when he noted the way Steve, now in his human form, marched over to Andrew and Don, who were still in their animal shapes.

"Your piece of shit brother tried to rape my mate. You're fucking right I made him regret it!"

Steve slammed his fist down onto Don's snout, and then he and Andrew worked together to maul the other shifter.

Were they going to kill him? Probably.

Don was right. Jonas was a subhuman, so he did know some of the basic rules. One of them was that you absolutely did not fuck with someone's mate.

Maybe they wouldn't kill him at all. If they wanted to. Don was doing his level best to fuck up their plans if that was the case. He clearly didn't want to be killed, and he fought and struggled with the other wolf shifters to make sure that didn't happen.

Even in the state he was in now, Jonas was angry

enough at this entire thing to kind of hope they succeeded.

Then, if Jonas' died, he could find Don on the other side and beat the piss out of him on an equal playing field.

He ignored the fight. There was no point in keeping his eye on it when there was someone much more important to look at right here.

"I'm sorry I couldn't keep you safe."

"Don't talk like that." Taylor faded in and out. She took off the shirt she'd been wearing, pressing it to Jonas' middle, and then he was struggling to stay awake while trying to tell her how much he loved her.

More shouting. He couldn't make out what was going on. Everything burned, and he didn't want to be here anymore. It was an eternity. It hurt so bad he didn't have the words to describe it.

Then, another small eternity later, the shouts and growls seemed to stop, and Steve was there.

"He's bitten pretty bad. In multiple spots," Steve said. The man stood over Jonas, looking down at him as though he were rotting meat that had fallen on his kitchen floor.

Not only did Jonas not like being looked at like that, but he wanted to know what the hell he was doing standing there.

When did he get the time to come over here? Shouldn't he be handing Don his ass to him? Jonas wanted to tell the man to mind his own business and get back to work, but now even his tongue felt heavy.

And Steve looked like absolute shit. So the fact that he could look down at Jonas like that spoke volumes.

"What should we do? Can we move him like this?"

Taylor sounded hysterical. He wanted to comfort her, to tell her it was fine. It didn't hurt. The rumors were true. It didn't hurt.

"We have to get him to the hospital. Right now."

"Wait, where's Don?"

"Don't try to talk, baby. Squeeze my hand, instead. Stay with me."

"Where's Don?" He couldn't let it go. They couldn't take him out of here until he knew, but Taylor seemed determined to make Jonas squeeze her hand, as though he would fade away if he didn't.

He tried, he really did, but he couldn't hold his focus for that long, and then Jonas did fade.

Jonas didn't remember anything else after that. He just knew that if Taylor started to cry over him, and Steve didn't kill Don for all those damned fires, then he was going to be pissed.

CHAPTER 29

Everything hurt. Everything throbbed. His body was on fire, and for a while, Jonas just wanted to end it. He swam in a sea of blackness. He couldn't see for miles in one way or another. He went under so many times it was a small miracle he didn't drown.

It felt like drowning, but at least if he were drowning, it would be in the water. This was not the water; this was something else. This didn't cool his heated body; it didn't put out the fire that burned the skin off his hands, legs, and arms.

He could see the bones of his fingers. The tips almost looked like claws.

He was subhuman. He didn't have claws. He didn't shift. He didn't…

Where was he again? Why did this hurt?

Fuck! Taylor! Meg!

He had to get to them. Had to find them. They could be lost in this inky black sea, and he couldn't let them drown, too.

He could hear her. Jonas could hear Taylor's voice. Close at times. So close he could reach out and almost touch her.

Other times, she sounded so far away it was clear he'd gone in the wrong direction to find her.

And the longer he couldn't find her, the more he wanted to roar. The more he wanted to tear himself out of his skin, to become a monster. To rip through anyone or anything that would get in his way.

It was hell. It was limbo, and he wanted to kill anyone who got in his way.

But it was only him. That was the part that was killing him.

When he opened his eyes, it was such a shock that it felt as though he'd been doused in the face with cold water. He didn't know where he was. Who he was. Bright lights and strange smells assaulted every sense he had.

The overwhelming flood of information hurt his eyes, his nose, and his brain. He couldn't stand it. He had to get out!

Wires poked and prodded at him from seemingly all angles. Something was in his nose. He pulled it out and felt the air change, not as crisp or clean, and the smells around him worsened.

Sharp needles were shooting up his nose. That was the only way to describe this.

Jonas rolled out of bed. An alarm sounded somewhere. His eardrums throbbed. Jonas clutched at his ears, but it was barely enough to stop the strange rush of pain that hit him.

People rushed into the room. Don's men. The wolves loyal to him.

They grabbed at Jonas' arms, issued commands, but he ignored them. He pulled at the people who attacked him. He threw them across the room and relished it when their bodies hit the walls.

They smelled strange. He wanted to tear them to pieces.

"Jonas, stop!"

There was only one person in the world that could make his body freeze like that. Jonas didn't move a damned muscle.

Her voice. It was amplified somehow. Taylor's voice always had a specific something to it that could make him stop in his tracks.

He turned towards the sound. The light in the bright room seemed to change when he spotted her. As if all that light was suddenly drawn to her, creating a sort of halo effect.

She looked worried. She looked very much alive. Her clothes were different than what she'd been wearing when they left her sloth.

Clean jeans and a loose white hoodie. Somehow, he could still make out every curve of her shape, from her breasts to her hips, and he wanted her.

So Jonas went to her, but his feet lost strength on the first step. He fumbled to his knees.

That was all right because Taylor was at his side in an instant. Her hands on him were a balm, unlike anything he'd ever felt before in his life.

"Easy, easy. I've got you."

He looked at her, touching her face, marveling at how she could be here.

She smiled back at him. "I missed you, too."

Jonas blinked. "Meg?"

"She's safe, she's fine. Don't you worry about a thing."

That relieved him, but Jonas still wished he could see his little girl. He wanted to confirm with his own eyes that she was all right.

"What happened?"

Taylor's dark eyes shone. "You're not going to believe this, but Andrew is alive. He's alive, Jonas."

Something within him sat up straight and howled. "That's…that's good news. Wow."

He was stunned. He didn't have the words to describe what exactly this meant.

Though he supposed it also made sense on another level.

Of course Andrew would be alive. It took so much more than that to take down a shifter. Especially a bear shifter.

"Wait, did I see him…was he at the…"

Taylor nodded. "I wasn't sure if you would remember that, or how much of it you'd even seen. You were so… Never mind. When his body recovered enough, and he finally woke up and saw we were gone, he came to find us. He helped Steve and Jackson defeat Don."

That didn't sound as though she were saying he was dead.

"Is he alive?"

Her expression changed. Jonas knew the answer at that moment, and he wanted to tear someone's head off for it.

"He's alive." It wasn't a question this time around. It was the truth. "They let him go?"

"No," Taylor shook her head. "It was just too much. He

weaseled his way out. They couldn't chase him down. Steve and Jackson didn't want to leave me by myself with you and Zelda, and Andrew was injured. He tried chasing Don down. He was pissed, but he came back only a few minutes later. He knew he couldn't chase after Don on his own."

Jonas looked up and around. The smells were still strong. The general vibe he got calmed to something more acceptable, and when he took note of the nursing staff all around him, some of whom he'd thrown at the wall, he couldn't help but feel ashamed for his actions.

"Come on, let's get you back into bed."

Jonas let Taylor help him to his feet. She eased him back into bed.

"I thought I was somewhere else," he muttered. Jonas couldn't help the rush of embarrassment that hit him now that he realized he'd attacked innocent people.

What the hell had he been thinking?

Taylor rubbed at his arm. That made it easier to let the staff come close and start poking at him again. They put everything back where it was supposed to go. They hooked him in, and then it felt like he was in a hospital again.

"I'm sorry."

Taylor frowned, staring at him. "For what?"

He wet his lips. "I thought I could keep you safe. There are so many times I could have gotten you out of there, but I didn't take any of those times. I just...fucked up at every step of the way."

Taylor was already shaking her head. Jonas didn't understand how she could be so forgiving. "Don't say things like that. You didn't fuck up. You protected me, you kept our little girl safe, and you saved the lives of all those people in the motel. I…" Taylor seemed to think over her next words. "I would have hoped you would want to take care of Meg as much as possible, but the fact that you would still do anything at all for me…after everything that happened."

Jonas grabbed her by her hand, holding onto it tight. He would have pressed his mouth to her knuckles if he didn't feel so out of it.

He held on tight instead. "I'd go to the damned moon and back for you. I love you."

Taylor inhaled a sharp breath. She cleared her throat.

"It's okay if you don't feel the same."

"That's not it," she said, still looking a little too sorry for his liking. "I just thought that, if when your painkillers wore off, when you were a little more focused, and your head wasn't so cloudy…"

"I'm perfectly wide awake right now. I even see the nurses over there as nurses. Not killer clowns with butcher knives."

She smiled at that. That was good. It was always better when he could pull a smile out of her.

Jonas closed his eyes. He could barely keep them open.

"Don't go anywhere. Be here when I wake up."

"Sure. I'll do that."

"You can say you love me back if you want to."

Taylor laughed again. She pulled her hand back long enough to wipe at her eyes. "You know I do."

"Good. Don't ever forget it." He raised a finger. "Or there will be hell to pay."

She laughed again. He felt her lean in, her perfect mouth covering his.

"All right, Prince Charming. You rest now. When you wake up, I will be here. I'll try to make sure Meg is here, too, but that one might get tricky, and when you get out of here, I'll be able to tell you about all the other things that happened. You're going to have to get used to this new shape you've got, and if you want me to, I can help you to control it."

Jonas wasn't sure he caught that last bit, but the only important thing he needed to know was that Taylor said she would be here. His daughter would be here, and they were…all right.

They would still get their chance. This wasn't over.

He could sigh and finally sleep easy knowing that much.

Everything else, as far as he was concerned, was filler.

The End

USA Today Bestselling Author Mandy Rosko is a videogame playing, book loving chick. She loves writing paranormal romances that range from light steamy to erotic, and has some contemporary and historical romances as well. You can find her on all sorts of platforms, including Twitch, Patreon, Wattpad, Radish, and more!

Get all the latest news from Mandy by signing up for her newsletter: http://eepurl.com/bQ8HvT

And get the most up-to date information on releases from Eighth Ripple Press by signing up for our newsletter: http://eepurl.com/gcUObH

facebook.com/MandyRoskoRomance

twitter.com/rizzorosko

instagram.com/mandyroskodraws

bookbub.com/authors/mandy-rosko

Vampires Don't Share with Dragons

Dangerous Guardian

Mate of a Dragon Villain

My Angel Lover Have Mercy on Me (M/M)

Bad Boy Billionaire Brothers

Arrangement with a Billionaire

Holiday with a Billionaire

The Billionaire's Fantasy